# PRAISE FOR RAVEN OAK

*With a ferocious-yet-fragile heroine, resonant themes, and a sweepingly gorgeous backdrop, Amaskan's Blood delivers food for thought and frank enjoyment."*

MAIA CHANCE, AUTHOR OF THE *FAIRY TALE FATAL SERIES*

*The prose itself is...a cut above the rest as Raven Oak playfully dances with the reader. It's the addition of just enough detail, and the right amount of it, that makes this read. Oak is loquaciously talented and the writing in the book shines. [She] crafts [her] words carefully, in order to pull the reader in, and once he's hooked, reels him in.*

OPEN BOOK SOCIETY

*The dialogue [in Amaskan's War] is authentic, the world is exquisitely depicted, and Margaret herself blossoms into a powerhouse before our very eyes. If there is such a thing as a "sloggy middle" when it comes to a series, it appears nobody told Raven Oak that.*

JAMIE MICHELE FOR READERS' FAVORITE

*[In Class-M Exile] Oak hurls you thousands of years into the future and hits you at the core of your being. It's a fresh look at science fiction in a charming "hillbilly" fashion... The plot has as much intrigue, suspense and action befitting a much larger work... a testament to Oak's skill at short fiction writing.*

OPEN BOOK SOCIETY

# DRAGON SPRINGS & OTHER THINGS

A Short Story Collection: Book I

## RAVEN OAK

GREY SUN
PRESS
BOTHELL, WA

# DRAGON SPRINGS & OTHER THINGS
## A Short Story Collection: Book I

Raven Oak

GREY SUN
PRESS

Grey Sun Press
PO Box 1635
Bothell, WA 98041




*Mirror Me,* 1st edition published in *Magic Unveiled Anthology* from Creative Alchemy, Inc. 2nd edition, Mercedes Lackey's *Fantasy Quarterly Magazine, Issue 0,* from Pulse Publishing.

*Alive,* 1st edition published in *Swords, Sorcery, & Self-Rescuing Damsels* from Clockwork Dragon Publishing.

*The Ringers,* 1st edition published in *Joy to the Worlds: Mysterious Speculative Fiction for the Holidays* from Grey Sun Press.

*Amaskan,* 1st edition published *Hidden Magic: Magic Underground Anthology* from Magical Mayhem Press.

*Peace be with You,* 1st edition published by Grey Sun Press.


Cover art by R. Oak




ISBN: 978-1-947712-06-5
Library of Congress Control Number: 2023938245

# TABLE OF CONTENTS

# MIRROR ME

uman waste and the sweet smell of blackberries mixed as a tech sawed at the brambles snagged in the dead guy's clothing. "Lucky that jogger's dog escaped," said Detective Frye at my shoulder. I turned away from the body but not before I caught a glimpse of his broad face, thinning eyebrows set over brown eyes, and chapped, generous lips. The face shifted for a moment as the "mirror" superimposed my face over the vic's.

I closed my eyes against the sight.

When I opened them, Frye chuckled. "Never seen you get queasy over a stiff before, Chandler."

I ignored the jibe and focused on the dozen officers canvassing the hobos dumb enough to stick around. More officers walked Rizal Park hoping to find a sober witness, but that seemed unlikely considering our proximity to the Jungle. Hundreds of dirty tents and cardboard hovels lay under the elevated section of I-5—home to a thousand transients. Nothing but an unsafe harbor of depravity and helplessness—one I avoided when I could.

Here, more than anywhere else, the "mirror" fell upon me, giving every hobo my face and serving me their drama on a painful platter.

The medical examiner tapped my shoe from where he squatted

beside the body, and I turned, careful to avoid looking at any faces. With the blackberries cut back, Dr. Moots shaded his eyes against the setting sun and pointed to a gunshot wound to the chest.

"Cause of death?" I asked.

"We'll know more after the autopsy."

My gaze slid upward. The vic's brown eyes disappeared in my own, which stared back at me without emotion. No pain or hunger. Just an emptiness that left me chilled in the shade of I-5.

Why now?

The "mirror" had left me alone for years. Left me to see people with their filter intact. But here, now, I couldn't tell where the vic's face began and mine ended. Dammit.

"Are you okay, Detective Chandler?" Moots asked.

"Yeah, I'm fine," I said before jotting down a few more details: the man's feet were bare, his Levi's a couple sizes too big, and his well-worn purple polo sported an alligator logo.

Ten feet away, a uniform chatted with the jogger whose inquisitive corgi whined. "We go to the park every evening to get in a few miles," the guy said, "but Ein slipped his leash when he spotted a cat. Or maybe a raccoon? Look, I don't know--he spotted something and was off. I followed him under the overpass until the blackberries. Darned things are impossible to get rid of. I thought Ein was snacking on them 'til I saw the dude's foot."

I didn't have to turn around to recall the teeth marks that marred the vic's feet, one big toe missing—presumably in the dog's stomach now.

The corgi whined as I approached, and the jogger flinched.

"Did you see anyone else?" I asked.

"N-no, just the dead guy. Look, when I saw Ein chewing on him—" The jogger paled and swallowed hard. "I just got the hell out of there and called you guys. I didn't see anybody except the usual homeless and dog walkers."

The uniform scribbled notes as his gaze flickered between the witness's face and mine. His feelings washed over me, and fear gripped my stomach. The uniform didn't want to be here. Not in the Jungle. Too much color for him.

I shook my head to clear my mind before shifting focus back to the jogger. "You'll need to keep a close eye on your dog's excrement when scooping. That toe's evidence, so if you find it, give us a shout."

The jogger looked like he was going to decorate the homeless encampment with his dinner. The officer glanced at his watch as he shifted his stance.

Shadows shifted as the Jungle's inhabitants watched us. We needed to talk to them, convince them we needed their help and weren't going to harm them.

But as the sun dipped closer to the horizon, people drifted away from the park. Once the sun set, no one would be safe in the Jungle.

Not even a dead guy.

THIRTEEN. THAT'S HOW OLD I'D BEEN THE FIRST TIME.

I'd turned the corner on my bike to find a homeless man shambling toward me, carrying a jar of something yellow. "Spare some change?" he'd asked, and I'd stood there blinking furiously against the way his face blurred. I'd still been able to see him, but my face was superimposed over his like I'd crossed my eyes funny.

His Vodka craving had swept over me, and shocked, I'd fallen to the pavement and scraped my knee. A nearby gas station attendant had chased the homeless man off with a slew of curse words.

Nothing else looked weird, so I had chalked it up to too much soda and sun. Until it happened again.

Soon I couldn't go anywhere without seeing this "mirror," as I'd dubbed it. My grades had dropped as I'd ditched school because there's nothing worse than a bunch of middle schoolers bleeding pain. Two weeks was all it took for my mother to weasel it out of me.

Her advice was, "Just close your eyes until it goes away."

The rest of seventh grade had been a montage of darkness. By the time I'd entered high school, I'd figured out that emotions fed it. If I wanted to survive it, I needed to remain numb.

So at eighteen, I'd entered the police academy with the goal of turning myself into a methodical, hardened cop as fast as I could.

Steeped in depravity, desperation, and violence, I'd figured I'd soon learn everyone was shit and cease to care. There weren't any innocent people in this world—only varying degrees of bad. But this vic—something about him brought the mirror back. Like the Terminator, it had resurfaced.

As I climbed the concrete incline of the Jungle, the shadows lengthened; something I'd mistaken for newspapers flapping in the wind stumbled away from me.

"Hey! Wait a minute!" I called out.

The newspaper-covered hobo glanced over his shoulder, nostrils flaring as he stopped and sniffed the air. "Got a smoke?" he asked.

"Sorry."

I touched his shoulder as he shuffled forward, and he spun around with a hiss. "Go 'way, fuzz."

"I just want to talk. Nothing else."

Newspaper guy continued to the top of the concrete hill, and when I followed him, hundreds of familiar brown eyes looked on me with contempt and mistrust. I closed my eyes to clear the mirror and something slammed into my shoulder, knocking me flat on my back. I gasped for air as someone shouted, "Ya'll better get gone. This here's ours."

By the time I caught my breath and sat up, the shadows had retreated and I was alone.

"Hey! Hey, Chandler!" Down the hill, Frye waved at me. "Got something!"

The trip down went faster than the climb up. Frye stood over a man in a dirt-smeared Seahawks jersey who leaned drunkenly against a fire hydrant. Grey dreds spilled out of his cap and when he smiled, a grill clung to what few teeth remained. I hesitated to meet his gaze, but when I did, he stayed him.

"Roberts here wanted to speak with you," said Frye. "Asked for you by name."

"Yeah, I did, didn't I?" Roberts raised his paper-bagged bottle in a toast. "You're Mickey's boy, you is. He always said you was fuzz. Ain't ever said you was so young!"

Damn fool laughed like a donkey. I asked, "Mickey who?"

"Mickey, Mickey, he so fine. He—"

"Frye?" I tilted my head towards the bottle. Frye took it from Roberts, who cried out. "You'll get it back," I said. "Who's Mickey? And why did you need me?"

Roberts closed his eyes. "Mickey is...Mickey. Michael Stevens."

I flinched. My mother had only said it the once, but I'd drilled my father's name into my five-year-old brain until it stuck. "What about him?"

"I just had to see for myself. You a good lookin' kid." Roberts grinned, then slumped over, snoring. I shrugged at Frye. I didn't know where Roberts had picked up the name, but he wasn't talking now. Damn drunk.

Frye flipped on his flashlight against the shadows that multiplied exponentially. "Getting late, man. We can come back tomorrow."

"Yeah. Tomorrow."

As I followed Frye, I glanced once over my shoulder. Just the once.

That was all it took for the mirror to settle over Roberts' face like a curse. I picked up the pace until we reached the squad car's safety.

⚜

The next morning, I brushed my teeth and shaved, then pressed my nose to the glass mirror. Nothing moved of its own accord, so I dressed as normal and headed to the West Precinct.

My ten-minute light rail commute was unremarkable. And, as usual, I tuned out the panhandlers and tech-bros on my five-minute walk to the cop shop. But the longhaired dude with a guitar and a sign reading "Anything helps, though weed helps more!" caught my attention— hazard of the job—and when I glanced his way, my own face wavered back at me, singing off-key.

I kept my head down after that, all the way to the precinct.

I was barely in the door when Frye caught my shoulder. "Moots has something for us," said my partner.

By the time we were rolling in his Ford Interceptor SUV, rain was sprinkling down. Typical.

"Did Moots find C.O.D.?" I asked as Frye drove.

"Didn't say. Just left a message to swing by A-SAP." Frye took a right on 9th where the guitarist had switched out his sign for one reading, "Seeking Sugar-Mama! Pretty, Ugly, Anything helps."

I closed my eyes against his hunger and the other shifting faces and didn't bother to open them until we pulled into another parking garage. I counted the sidewalk lines as we walked to the building and stared at the elevator doors as we rode up to the second floor.

An assistant waved us in the direction of the morgue—our home away from home. Inside, Moots leaned over a corpse. "...Ligament is detached from the femur. STOP." A short beep sounded, and he removed his gloves before walking us over to our victim.

I kept my eyes on the sleeve of Moot's scrubs as he pulled back the sheet.

"The deceased was shot three times, once each to the chest, stomach, and left shoulder. Based on the angles of entry, there were multiple shooters." Moots lifted the man's left shoulder and pointed. "This shot came from behind." He let the body down. "But cause of death was one of the two anterior shots. One bullet hit the aorta before nicking the left lung. He bled out quickly. Time of death between 6 and 8 P.M."

"Do we have an ID?" Frye asked, and the M.E. pointed to a tattoo on the man's forearm. I leaned over the three conjoining circles.

*You're Mickey's boy, you is.*

"Tattoo of the famous mouse, eh? Shoulda stayed in mouse land." Frye's joke mixed with Roberts' voice, scattering my thoughts. The victim's shaggy, gray beard needed a good trim and the lines around his eyes carried a sadness even post-mortem. Now that I'd expected the mirror, it didn't manifest. It didn't need to.

"You okay, Chandler?" my partner asked.

"Yeah. Just an odd tattoo for a bum, is all."

Moots nodded. "His prints weren't in the system, so I put in a call to Detective Juarez in Outreach, who recognized our victim by the tattoo. The name's Michael Stevens aka Mickey. He was in and out of the mental health system. Heavy drinker according to his liver."

Frye shrugged. "Not all these guys brush with the law, though it certainly makes me wonder what he did to get all shot up."

"Or how he avoided a public intoxication charge. Thanks, Moots," I said as I turned away from my father.

Before I returned to the Jungle, I'd have to make another stop: My momma's. I hadn't been there often enough lately.

MOMMA'S HOUSE WAS A CONSTANT IN SEATTLE'S EVER-changing landscape. Tucked between a dog park and a high-rise condo, her blue cottage was one of the few remaining single-family homes left in the Central District. A startled shout answered my knock.

The door creaked open, and my momma smiled out at me. "Dane Michael Chandler, you get yourself inside before you let out all the cool air!"

I smiled at her as she walked her five-foot-nothing-self barefoot across the threadbare carpet towards the kitchen. Nothing about the way she moved spilled the secrets of her health, but the rattling window unit was a harsh reminder. "Sorry it's been so long since I came by," I said as ice cubes clinked into a glass from the kitchen.

She returned holding a glass of tea and thrust it at me with a pout. "Shouldn't take a hot day to get my boy back home, but I see you wearin' a tie so this ain't a social call neither. Where's your partner? That fool roastin' in that tank out there?" She pulled back the curtain to peer outside. "Damn fool. You tell him to get his butt in here--"

"Momma, he's fine. I gotta ask you some questions about...about Mickey."

The one face that never changed, never mirrored, lost its smile, and Momma settled into her recliner with a sigh. "Been a long time since we talked 'bout him." Her wrinkled hand, still cool from the iced glass, touched my cheek as her eyes narrowed. "It's back, ain't it? That mirror?"

"Yeah, but that's not the reason I came over." I took a swallow of tea before continuing. "Momma, Mickey's dead."

I waited for some outcry of grief or anger—anything—but she merely shrugged. "Don't you go expectin' tears, baby. Mickey ain't been welcome in this house since the day he left. I ain't mournin' what I lost a long time ago."

"You don't want to know how he died?"

"Was it that mirror?" she asked, and I shook my head. "Then I don't care one way or the other."

"He was shot, Momma. Can you think of any reason—"

"No."

"When he was—when you two were still together, did he ever talk about the mirror?"

An ice cube popped in my glass, but my momma just stared at the front door.

"Far as I know, it was always with him, even when we met. Some days he was Mickey. Others, he was lost in what he saw and felt. Was like that the day you were born." Conflicted, muddy eyes turned to me. "Whatever he saw, he was never the same after he looked at you."

So I *was* the reason he'd left. Me...and the mirror. "When I look at folks, I see me. Feel their pain, their hunger and helplessness like it's mine."

"What about their happiness? Their excitement and wonder?"

"Maybe long ago, but it all bleeds together after a while." I set my glass down and strode over to the door. "Mickey was right. Maybe it *is* easier to forget pain inside a bottle."

She moved mighty fast for a lady of seventy as she caught my cheek. "Mickey ain't ever had anything right. Now you go be the man he wasn't—go catch his killer—, 'cause you ain't no mirror, Dane. No you ain't."

I kissed Momma on her forehead before I left. I had a crime to solve, whether I ended up like Mickey or not.

"YOUR MOM HAVE ANY INSIGHT INTO OUR CASE?"

I ignored Frye's sarcasm as I drove up I-5 towards the Jungle. "Nah, but Roberts—now he's a guy who might know something."

"How you figure?" asked Frye.

"He mentioned the vic when we were at the scene."

My partner frowned, then inhaled swiftly through his nose. "The dude with the dreds, right? He said—sonofabitch. Is that why we visited your mom's?"

I nodded as I took the Jackson Street exit. "She hasn't seen him since I was three. Me neither, but I figured it was worth a shot."

Frye was thinking awfully hard judging by the way his eyebrows tried to touch the bridge of his nose, but he remained silent until we parked and got out.

"You gonna tell the lieutenant 'bout your pop?"

"I didn't even know the man. No point in making waves when there isn't any water."

But I couldn't shrug it off so easily; every time I caught a glimpse of others around me, their faces were my own. My father's death had me spinning. If the lieutenant removed me from the case, the damned mirror might never go away again, and I'd be as useless as Mickey.

Once we were spotted, a few figures of the Jungle faded into the background, though there weren't many people here this time of day. A dozen or so transients remained under blanket tents in the overpass's shade. A few used their hats as fans, and some lay, eyes closed, as they slept through the day's rising heat. Frye nudged me and nodded to my right where Roberts flipped cards one at a time across a cardboard box.

"Roberts, it's Detective Chandler. We spoke the other day about—"

"You think I don't remember Mickey's kid?" He wheezed between guffaws. "I knew you'd be back. You play Texas Hold 'em? Game was Mickey's favorite."

My partner shrugged out of his jacket, which he spread across the warm pavement. "We got time for a hand or three."

Roberts shuffled his ragged cards. I folded to the ground as the cards were dealt, and Roberts' gaze flickered between the two of us. "Cards were never my thing," I said, closing my eyes a moment.

Frye and Roberts played for twenty minutes while I stewed in my button-up shirt with rocks poking through my jacket. Just when I thought I might melt, Roberts flipped over his whole hand. "Four-of-a-kind," he said, his ragged smile nearly as brown as his skin.

"Bust," said Frye as he flipped over matching aces. "Looks like you win."

Roberts turned my way with his own face. "You got questions 'bout Mickey."

"You mentioned him the day we found his body." When he nodded, I asked, "Were you here when he was shot?"

"You ain't gonna ask 'bout your dad none?"

"What's there to ask?"

Roberts retrieved an old compact mirror from a ratty pocket. Maybells. Same powder my momma used.

He handed it to me and said, "Open it."

Taped to the cracked mirror inside was a thumb-sized photo I hadn't seen before. A much younger, happier Mickey held baby me in front of him. I was reaching for him, my little hand grabbing hold of his nose.

"He looked in that mirror every night," said Roberts.

"I'm surprised he could look in a mirror at all." I swallowed back a wave of emotions. When he'd looked in the mirror, who had looked back? Rust flaked along the mirror's edge along with something else rust-colored. "This might be blood," I said. Frye bagged the compact as I looked back at Roberts. "Mickey had it the night he died, didn't he?"

Roberts nodded. "They tried to nick it, they did, but Mickey wouldn't let 'em. That's all he had."

"You said 'they.' Did you see who shot Mickey?"

The homeless man stuffed his cards in his pocket with a frown. "Don't be askin' me to snitch. The Jungle take care of its own. 'Sides, if you didn't know Mickey like you says, what you care?"

Frye's cell buzzed, and he said, "We're needed back at the precinct."

I handed a business card to Roberts. "I don't matter, but if you really care about Mickey, you'll want justice. Show this card on the 36 bus, and it'll get you to me."

Roberts shoved the business card into the same dirty pocket as his playing cards. I didn't need a mirror to sense his pain. "Mickey was a good 'un. Mighta been crazy, but there were moments when he saw *me*.

Moments he looked at me just like you lookin' right now. But that's all I can do for you both."

He shuffled off, and my partner shrugged. "You can lead a horse to water...."

Except this horse knew something. Being cold and impartial kept me sane, kept me from seeing a mirror in every face and every victim, but this victim had a name I knew. In saving him, I might save me. One way or the other, I had to get Roberts to talk.

A shooting at the U-Dub campus kept Frye and me hopping the next few days, though when Mickey crept into conversation, the mirror wavered across everyone I saw, shifting them from anonymous strangers into people whose intimate secrets were now my own. My face on murderers and victims, helpless students, harried cops and horrified parents.

An email caught me in a rare moment at my desk. The lab had pulled partial prints off Mickey's compact. Aside from mine, all the prints belonged to people from the Jungle: Roberts, Mickey, and a teenager by the name of Terence Pickett with a short record of drug possession arrests. The blood, however, had been Mickey's.

"Yo, Frye. You see this?"

My partner glanced up from his computer screen. "Yeah. T's been on Narcotics' radar for a few years now. Rumor is he's looking to upgrade from runner to dealer."

Behind Frye, a uniformed officer escorted Roberts in from the elevator. His right eye was swollen shut, and a trickle of blood had dried on his cheek. He kept his eyes down as the officer led him to an interrogation room. I caught Frye's eye, and we followed them.

Roberts scratched at his cut-up knuckles as we entered the room. I chased off the uniform with a look, then took a seat across the table. "You want to talk about that eye?" I asked.

"Stupid punk. Ain't nothin'."

Frye set a glass of water beside Roberts then sat beside me. The homeless man finished the water, then crumpled the paper cup in his hands. "I didn't wanna come, but punk left me no choice. He ain't from the old Jungle. Don't understand her rules."

Frye and I exchanged a look. Survival of the fittest ruled there, at least as far as SPD was concerned. I waited another beat or two before asking, "You mind if we record you?"

Roberts nodded, but not before levying a distrustful glare at the camera. "All right. I seen Mickey get shot. Was cool that night so we was all lyin' around. Mickey'd scored some dough and we was havin' us a can of baked beans when them two rolled up."

"Who?" Frye asked.

"One of 'em goes by T. Don't know the other one, but T I know. He's trouble with a T." Roberts laughed a moment, then continued. "They got some fancy bikes, wanted Mickey's cash, but he ain't hand it over. T made a grab for it and knocked Mickey on his ass. Made him empty his pockets."

I asked, "Did T take the compact?"

"Minute he touched it, Mickey went crazy. I ain't ever seen nothing like it—he a wild man. Go to jump them punks, but they was strapped."

"Did you see them shoot Mickey?" I asked.

Roberts nodded. "Mickey started runnin' and T shot him from behind. When Mickey went down, I hid in a bush, but I seen T yell at the younger one. Told that kid to shoot Mickey or else, so that kid did it. Then he done shot him again. And Mickey stayed down."

His fear shook me deep in the belly, and I closed my eyes against the mirror.

"Don't close your eyes to it, son. That's what took Mickey. Took his mind."

My eyelids snapped open. Roberts reached his shaking hand across the table to pat mine. "You try and shut out the world, and the world will swallow you."

"I'm not the mirror."

"That what you call it?" he asked, and I nodded. "You ain't the mirror. Mickey weren't neither."

"It doesn't freak you out?"

"Been livin' in the Jungle for most my life. Seen a lot of weird shit, but Mickey's mirror...nah. Kinda makes some weird sense, y'know?"

Frye cleared his throat. "I'm not gonna ask. Roberts, could you ID these guys from a photo lineup?"

"I'd know T and that kid anywhere. Gimme them photos." Roberts smiled a sad little smile at me and patted my hand again. "You still owe me another card game, Mr. Chandler."

My partner glanced at the video camera on his way to the door. The moment he was gone, I said, "I'll do better than that. How about one of my momma's home cooked meals and a card game?"

"It's a date."

FRYE AND I SPOTTED T NEAR 10TH AND DEARBORN. THE SUN set behind the overpass as we followed him on foot to an abandoned van. We used a park fence for cover as T got inside. The Chevy's fading white paint had grown spots of primer, and the plates had been removed, but the description fit a meat packing truck stolen last year.

As we crouched outside, a metallic object crashed inside the van. "Dammit. You clumsy shit," someone hissed, followed by an unintelligible whisper.

"Van's on city property," Frye whispered.

I sent him around back, gun drawn, while I trained my sights on the side door. When I threw it open, Terence stood in the hollowed out van with a soda can in his hand, carbonation running over its edge. A younger teen held a wad of damp paper towels.

"What the fuck man!" Terence yelled.

I kept my gun on Terence while pulling my badge. I hadn't even flipped it open before Terence darted for the van's rear. Frye tapped his gun against the rear window, and Terence stopped, eyes wide. He whipped his head back and forth between us.

The younger teen dropped the paper towels.

"Police. Put your hands up," I shouted as Frye came through the rear.

Terence tried to duck around Frye, who caught him with one arm and shoved him to the van's floor. The younger kid threw his hands in the air, eyes wide. We secured both of them in the SUV.

They argued while Frye searched the van in gloves. When he held up a 9mm Ruger, the punks' gazes mirrored my own. Their guilt and fear cut me like a sharp razor. Only a flash, but it was enough.

Frye took Terence into one interrogation room while I left his buddy—who called himself "K-dog"—in another. "K's" driver's license on the other hand, IDed him as Kristopher Mesmer. He'd stewed in his own sweat for a few hours while techs processed the van and Ballistics identified the gun as our murder weapon. The second weapon was still missing.

Kristopher's camo jacket was draped over the chair's back, leaving his long blonde hair to cling to his stained tank top. His gaze darted back and forth between me and the file folder on the table while I ignored them both. "You gonna ask me shit or what?" he asked.

"If you like, Kristopher."

His name set him squirming in his chair, and when I didn't grill him right away, he yelled, "Get on with it or lemme go. I got rights. And if you ain't gonna call me K-dog, the name's Kris."

The door behind him opened to a shriveled up lady pushing eighty and wearing a bun tighter than a wine cork. "Mr. Mesmer, my name is Elaina McMathan," she said as she claimed the empty chair beside Kris. "I'm from social services. I'm here in loco parentis."

"In loco what? You here 'cause my parents gone?" Kris asked.

"In loco parentis means that I am acting in place of your parents to ensure your rights aren't violated while in police custody."

"Get me outta here then. I didn't do nothing, I swear."

Ms. McMathan frowned as I opened the file folder and pulled out the ballistics report. I set a photo of Mickey's corpse in front of him. "You have few options, Mr. Mesmer," I said. "The gun we found in the van—"

"Ain't mine. Found it when we crashed in that van."

"—matches the slugs pulled from Mr. Stevens' body. Your prints are the only ones on the gun, and a witness has identified you as one of the shooters."

"What witness? That old man with the cards? Man, T said he wouldn't snitch—" Kris snapped his mouth shut, and the social worker leaned over to whisper something in his ear. The boy shook his head once before scowling at me. "I wanna deal."

I set a blank piece of paper before him but withheld the pen. "Where's the second gun?"

Kris shrugged.

"If you want a deal, you're going to have to give us that second gun," I said.

"And flip on T? He'll kill me."

"Terence is off the hook." The little lie fell heavy on my tongue as the boy's face fell. *Stop. I have work to do.* I had my eyes half-closed when Roberts' voice echoed back at me.

*Don't close your eyes to it, son.*

I opened my eyes to the mirror. "Terence's prints aren't on the gun. He's said it was all your idea. That you shot Mickey."

Kris lunged to his feet and strode over to the one-way window. He pounded on it with his fists and shouted, "You son-of-a-bitch, T! This was your play! Yours!"

"Sit down, Mr. Mesmer. He's not there," I said.

He shuffled back over to the table, red-faced and breathing hard. "He really gonna walk?"

I nodded. "If you work with us, we can keep this in juvenile court. But prison on Terence's behalf? I think you're smarter than that."

The eyes pleading with me weren't Kris's green, but Mickey's brown. The same brown in mine. Kid was guilty, but he was also just a kid.

Ms. McMathan whispered something else in his ear and Kris said, "The other gun—the one T used—is in the brush at the southwest corner of the park. T tossed it after the shooting."

"Why didn't you toss yours?" I asked.

"T's always sayin' I'm stupid. Guess I am."

He didn't feel stupid. His stomach felt tied in knots, and I shook my head. "I can't help you if you're not honest."

His face flushed. "T gets mad sometimes. Hits me. So I thought I might need it."

"Like you did with your dad?"

I didn't know why I said it, but Kris leaned back in his chair. "How'd you know?" he whispered.

His memories flooded my thoughts. The booze, his sister's broken arm, the gun. "Self-defense, Kris, and you had to protect your sister, right?" I slid the pen across the table. "Write down what happened. Both then and now."

Tears welled in Kris's eyes when his face returned. "T told me I had to shoot him. I didn't wanna do it. I swear."

I wanted to hate him for killing Mickey, but I couldn't. He was just a scared kid, like I'd been once.

*Don't close your eyes to it, son.*

For the first time, I wanted to see.

A

ABOUT "MIRROR ME"

Originally published in the *Magic Unveiled Anthology* (Creative Alchemy, Inc. ) and reprinted in *Issue 0* of Mercedes Lackey's *Fantasy Quarterly Magazine*, "Mirror Me" came from a discussion with my partner about the idea of crime. Nothing about crime is black and white. For example, most of us wouldn't imprison someone for stealing bread to feed their child, even though the law states that theft is illegal. But what if we saw ourselves in everyone? Could you punish a man who steals to eat if he looked like you? I decided to explore that on a literal level with our Seattle PD officer. Maybe if SPD had a mirror, they wouldn't be in constant trouble for corruption. Maybe we wouldn't have so many instances of police shooting innocent people...

# WATER THE FIRE

"You should hire an exorcist."

It was a phrase I heard a lot, especially seeing as this was the tenth time—wait, eleventh or was it twelfth? I shook my head. It didn't matter. If my house flooded one more time, we'd be making canoes in order to reach the kitchen.

I was twenty-four years old the first time the water demons attacked—a flood by way of a feuding couple in the apartment upstairs. Normal couples might shout or throw socks at one another, but these two were a bomb waiting to go off. Apparently, in the mind of the wife, payback involved water—specifically, toilet water.

Come 5 A.M., she stuffed their toilet full of paper, maxipads, and whatever else she could get her hands on. Then *geronimo!* She flushed it and left the apartment. The poor toilet did what any decent toilet would. It gave up the ghost and sent water everywhere. Of course, it wasn't clean toilet water but the mess after someone eats too many bean burritos. After all, everything's bigger in Texas!

Imagine waking before sunrise to a dresser being thrown out the window, followed by paint cans splattering paint across your window. The proverbial dust settled and as I stepped into the hall to call the landlord, shit-colored sludge poured through my light fixtures, coloring my white walls a smelly brown.

It's not a great way to play nice with the neighbors, that's for sure.

Prior to this, I'd been privy to the usual home drama like sinks clogging and the like. We'll call it a side effect of cheap, college town apartments. But there's an overflowing toilet and then here's *this*. Less *incident* and more like a disaster.

I figured it a one off. I mean, how many times do you end up with destructive neighbors such as this? But it doesn't take a bad neighbor for bad events to find you.

Five years later, I found myself in a new rental house. Texas heat coupled with a long day of moving way-too-many book boxes left me exhausted. All I wanted was air conditioning and some sweet tea.

I wasn't even gone an hour. Forty-five minutes tops, I swear.

That was all it took for the hot water heater to burst. I opened my front door to five inches of water. Soggy boxes stared back at me, their corners drooping like frowns. *Damn. Do I really have water demons?*

The next few hours were a blur of tossing boxes outside into the sun in a wild panic. The sun would save some of my belongings but not enough. While I'd wanted to replace some of my old and tattered books, a flood was not the method I would've chosen. At the time, two disasters seemed horrible, but they could reasonably be chalked up to normal life.

Over the next decade, water demons haunted us. Hot water heater failures, hailstorms punching holes in the roof and windows, flash floods, and one busted sewage pipe. *(What is it with me and sewage!?)*

The way I saw it, something was terribly wrong with me.

Maybe it was the state I lived in. I mean, maybe Texas was occupied by more water demons than other areas of the country. Maybe if I moved somewhere else, I could leave my demons behind, so when the opportunity presented itself, we packed up and moved to Washington State.

I know what you're thinking here. I'm haunted by water demons, and I *choose* to move to a rainy state. But there's a method to my thinking, I promise. Texas is hot. If anything, it should be controlled by something that meshes well with heat, like say a fire demon. My experiences said otherwise. If water demons held Texas in their grasp, perhaps a rainy state like Washington would be neutral territory.

We survived the first year. No demons. No water disasters. Nada. The second year, we weren't so lucky.

Seeing as how Seattle's expensive, we lived in a condo. Some people find them annoying from a noise perspective, but the view of Puget Sound made it worth it. While I work from home, sometimes it's nice to get out of the house and see actual people, i.e. those not inside a computer. I worked in one of my favorite haunts until it was time to head home and feed *los gatos*.

Inside the condo, water covered the floor. It covered the walls and the ceiling. Everywhere I looked, there was water, sixty-five gallons to be exact.

My upstairs neighbor's water heater had failed, and when I say failed, I mean the water in it swept into my home like a freaking tsunami. Paint bubbled and peeled from the moisture, while my gorgeous hardwood floors buckled and warped. The closet door was already trying to rust shut.

To fix the damage, we had to vacate our home and live in a temporary place while insurance contracted to gut the walls and flooring. New wood and drywall installed, walls replaced and painted, the works. But before that, they brought in the drying machines. If you've never seen them, they're like angry, evil fans the size of small cars that eat moisture for breakfast. They remove the humidity and moisture by making it *hot*. By burning the air.

In other words, they brought in fire demons to eat our water demons.

Of course, nothing's ever that simple with me. We were deemed "high risk" by insurance companies over too many claims. It didn't matter that none of these instances were our fault or even in our control. I certainly couldn't tell them about my water demon theory—not if I wanted to maintain ownership of my home. When I wasn't fighting insurance, I was dreaming—nightmares from childhood when fire burned down homes and businesses around me, leaving nothing remaining but ash and twisted, melted plastic.

I think I found myself thankful that our third year in Seattle was the year of the drought. The ground cracked and tree roots exposed themselves to the sun in hopes that some semblance of moisture would touch them. Marvelous evergreens shifted to brown in a city nicknamed the Emerald City, and everyone's lawn resembled Texas more than Washington State.

By the end of September, the return of the rainy season brought relief, then terror as downpours resulted in mudslides and flash floods. Despite how media portrays it, Seattle is a land of gentle mists and rain. It certainly rains most days of the year, but the amounts are much less than rain received elsewhere. Most days, a quarter-of-an-inch of rain in twenty-four hours warrants a flood watch. By contrast, six inches is considered a decent amount of rain in Texas.

I suppose I'm to blame for lamenting the loss of a good thunderstorm. Heavy rains swept across the area, dumping inches of rain in a short period of time. Soil meant for gentle mists and moss wasn't ready for this. With nowhere to go, water ran everywhere else, including down the sloped driveway at my new house. *(Oh yeah, Seattle is filled with hills. Not little ones either—we're talking tiny mountains here.)*

Our drainage couldn't keep up with the deluge. Before I could do more than blink, my garage was flooded and water had seeped into our foundation, where it oozed up through our basement flooring. Kitty paws freshly out of the litter box left muddy litter trails across the utility room as they ran for the safety of drier carpet.

"Is this normal?" I asked my neighbor.

When she nodded, a bad feeling returned to the pit of my stomach. Apparently, the neighborhood designers didn't think about proper drainage. Most owners had long since installed sump pumps in the basement and proper drainage around the entire property.

Drainage issues conquered, I begged the water demons to leave. If I could go a year without property damage, I could die happy.

Almost a year later to date, I came home to a basement full of water. *What the hell?* I thought. We'd already dealt with the drainage. It hadn't rained all week so how was there a flood?

The bottom three steps were soaked through, as were my socks once I stepped down. The carpet splashed as I walked, but what had leaked?

A peek into the closet beneath the stairs revealed standing water, but the utility room was dry, meaning it wasn't the water heater. The basement bathroom was also dry.

Despite it being a weekend, I called a plumber. Always my first step when I suspect water demons are making my life miserable. A man with a hefty beard and jeans that slid down to expose the traditional plumber's crack poked and prodded at carpet and walls. He crawled into closets and poked more holes. "Is there a bathroom down here?" he asked.

I nodded, pointing towards my nice, comfy bathroom. *(For reasons I'll never understand, the nicest bathroom in the house is indeed in our basement.)*

More poking and prodding.

How could he determine anything without knocking holes in the tile?

It didn't matter. "Your shower pan's failed," he said as he hitched up his pants. "You see, when it fails, there's no basin for the water to sit in while it drains. Instead, it runs for the nearest exit, whatever holes or tears develop in the pan. Then the water seeks a way out be it your drywall, flooring, and anywhere else it can find to go. You should call your insurance company."

Sunday night was a long conversation with an agent who wanted nothing more than to open yet another water damage claim on my account.

"We need our assessor to check it out and ensure there is actual damage to the home."

Yeah, they said that.

They also dispatched a water restoration company with their dutiful assessor. Both arrived at the same time and agreed with Sir Plumber that yes, the shower pan had failed. Half the basement would need to be gutted to the studs and rebuilt.

But first, they brought in the fire demon drying machines. Plastic barriers blocked off access to the basement as walls were opened up, carpet ripped apart, and custom Italian tile shattered into dust. The renovation took a year and once again, our water demons were vanquished.

But how long would they be gone? How long until they returned and yet another insurance company dropped us like a bad habit? None of the major companies would touch me, leaving me with only high risk policies, but what happened if I became too dangerous for even them? Who would protect me?

I had no other choice but to call in an expert. An exorcist.

He arrived on a Sunday morning while the rains remained in the mountains, leaving my town a warm summer day. "It's better this way," he explained as he walked around my property. "Rainy days are their days. The power shifts to them, which we don't want. Not if we're to take care of your problem."

"Makes sense."

"When is your birthday?" he asked.

"December."

"A child of fire, yes?"

I nodded.

"December is the sign of Sagittarius, protected by the element of fire. It makes some sense for the water demons to wish to take down a child of fire, but your experiences...are you someone of great importance?"

"Not that I know of."

He pursed his thin lips together and lay a hand on my forehead. "No, not important enough for such an onslaught."

*Gee, thanks. Not important enough, huh?*

He explored the yard first, touching the evergreens and the rose bushes and hydrangeas with his bare, weathered hands before heading inside. He lay his hands across one doorway and another, eyes closed. Then he moved toward the fireplace. "Do you use this?"

"Most winters."

He remained there for a solid ten minutes, mumbling under his breath.

When he opened his eyes, I asked, "What were you doing?"

"Communing with the house spirits," he said as if that explained everything.

See, I don't really believe in spirits and demons—maybe that was my problem—but at this point, I was willing to try anything to get rid of the water issues that had followed me since I'd moved away from Florida, land of sun and fire.

As he moved through my home, touching this and that, he continued to mumble in some unrecognizable language until we reached the basement. He turned suddenly to face me, his brows bunched up. "You've had electrical issues here, yes?"

"When we first moved in. The previous homeowner was supposed to fix them but didn't. She...uh, she lied. The house almost burned down from how everything was 'repaired.'"

He nodded and moved on, speaking to the hot water heater, the dryer, and the HVAC system. His hands ran along the walls from power outlet to power outlet until he'd touched every plug. "Tell me about your childhood. Where did you grow up? Have you ever had a house burn down or a hurricane take out your home? A tornado? Anything involving weather or elements?"

"I grew up all over. Where do you want me to start?"

"At the beginning."

"Okay..." It seemed like an odd question, but what did I know of exorcisms. "I was born in California—"

"A neutral state."

"A what?" I asked.

"Neutral states are places where all elements exist in equality. California has water in its ocean, earth in its earthquakes, fire in its warm sun, and air in its snowy peaks. Continue."

"We moved around a lot, but I spent most of my childhood in Florida and Texas." When he motioned for me to continue, I said, "In Florida, I swam a lot in the Atlantic Ocean. I was a water baby when it came to swimming, but there were several fires there. Apartment buildings next to ours burned down but never ours. We survived Hurricane Andrew and a few other hurricanes."

He lay his hands on the floor, his ear tilted toward it as he listened. "Interesting. What about Texas?"

"The Gulf Coast is nothing like the Atlantic. I've been a few times but never enjoyed it. Spent some time in pools but honestly, Texas is too hot. Too easy to sunburn. I've survived several tornadoes and windstorms with repairable damage to homes and objects but never any damage to my person."

He picked up his clipboard and glanced at it. "And your parents were born in states of Air and Fire. Interesting."

When he stood, he walked another loop around the house's interior, then took a seat on my couch.

Was he going to do an actual exorcism here? When was the magic or whatever going to happen that would save me from these water demons or whatnot?

He motioned for me to join him, and I chose the chair beside the couch. "What do we do next?" I asked.

"Nothing. You don't need an exorcism."

"I'm confused. When I first explained the issue, you thought it sounded exactly like that's what I needed."

"Yes, but since exploring your home and speaking with it, I've learned that I was wrong. See, you were born of fire, from parents of fire and air. This can lead to an imbalance as fire is dominant. Florida is a state of fire and water, while Texas is of fire and air, leading to further imbalance. You suffered traumatic experiences with fire as a child as well."

"Not directly."

"Exactly. Because you are a child of fire, it burned you but did not destroy you. Same with the air in Texas. It lifted you but did not sweep you away."

"Huh. I'd never thought of it like that," I said.

He nodded his head. "Most people don't. That's why they call me."

"But that still doesn't explain all the trouble I've had with water."

This time he smiled rather than remaining stern. "While you were born a child of fire, your love of water puts you in conflict with your sign. Your devotion to water has shifted you to be of water and no longer of fire. But fire's special. Like all elements, it can be both destructive and creative, but fire is how we are born. It is the symbol of eternal birth as we are made of stardust. From the fires we were formed and from the fires we crawled. For you to leave that which made you is a betrayal of the deepest kind."

He touched my forehead with his thumb. "Inside, you are

conflicted. To believe or not to believe. To go or to stay. To swim or to burn."

The way he explained it made an odd sort of sense. If I was now of water, why were they attacking me? Shouldn't they be leaving me alone? I said as much, and my exorcist laughed.

"If only it worked that way. The problem isn't in what's happening, but in how you're viewing it. You're seeing the water demons as attacking you, but that's not true. See, every instance where you'd suffered a flood or some other perceived water attack, it's been your water demons surrounding you and protecting you from the fire demons who feel betrayed. Your fire demons are angry with you, so they keep trying to stir chaos in your life. Your electrical system here at the house, for example.

"Your fire demons wished to burn your home to the ground. They don't feel you deserve a home after shifting who you are so easily. Rather than let the fire demons succeed, your water demons went to battle for you. The unfortunate side-effect of this was flooding your garage and basement. I'd wager that if you were to go back through every instance where water damaged your home, you'd find a connected experience where fire's involved."

My brain scurried back into my memories. The time the building beside us burned down, followed up by Hurricane Andrew. The time a fan caught on fire, followed by the toilet overflowing. Each instance, each moment where I thought the water demons hated me, easily connected to a time when fire wished to remove me from the Earth.

"Wow. I-I hadn't realized this connection until now. I think you might be right."

"Of course. It's my job to discover these connections. I suspect if you pay your water demons a bit more attention, you might run into less collateral damage when they are busy defending you."

He stood, using the couch's arm to steady himself. I could've sworn he had been taller when he'd arrived, almost as if the experience had sapped the energy from him, leaving him hunched over and tired.

"What do I owe you?" I asked as he moved towards the door.

"Nothing. I performed no exorcism here today."

I shook my head. "But you spent a long time talking to things and... Surely that's worth charging for."

He stood in the front door frame, his feet braced in the corners and his hands pressed against the sides. For a moment, he appeared to glow, then the shimmery haze was gone. "It is and it was," he said. When he stood, his height had returned as had all color to his face.

I didn't understand what he'd taken from my house, but it had reenergized him. My house had paid my debt, and I mumbled a brief thanks beneath my breath.

He nodded encouragingly before he left.

I followed him out where he hiked up our steep driveway and out to the road. There was no car or truck parked alongside our house, and I watched as he hiked down the road toward the evergreens at our street's dead end.

He gave a final wave before disappearing into the trees.

Whether or not I chose to believe it all, something had changed in the house. Something had changed in me. I think I had finally watered the fire.

### About "Water the Fire"

This story is part fact and part fiction as I've had quite the love-hate relationship with both fire and water in my life. Way too many close calls and destruction. Most of my friends have encouraged me to hire an exorcist in hopes my home will stop trying to flood me out, and I'll be honest—I considered it—but something told me that maybe, just maybe, that water was acting for good. Thus, a story was born.

# ALIVE

Black hair, blue eyes, tall frame for a girl. Throat slit ear-to-ear. The newest victim could've been a younger version of me, a *much, much* younger version if I ignored the number of silver hairs on my forty-five-year-old head. As King Leon's *sepier*, gathering information was what I did best as an all-around spy and problem solver, but a string of deaths—all women—had pulled me back toward Justice and the town of Loughrie.

As I stood outside the Merc's Guild, my neck throbbed in response to the report in my hands. I could feel the knife against my throat all over again. Had these women known their attacker? Had they struggled, as I had, or had their lives been over in a single gasp? The report sent to the King stated the Merc's Guild had handled the burning of all four victims, though they hadn't bothered reporting the murderers to the crown. Curious that they'd covered up their burning, leaving someone else to report it. The decision left me wishing I were back in Alexander rather than staring down my past.

It couldn't be coincidence that this girl looked like me.

The change in Loughrie was obvious in the line of mercs outside. Not one of 'em a woman, and none of 'em young. I nodded to 'em before glancing over their heads at the newly posted jobs. Caravan guards. One call for an archer at the border. None of it complicated, and none of it local.

I passed through the open door into the Guild itself where a whip of a girl scurried over. "Welcome to the Mercenary Guild. Fair work for fair pay. Are you lost?"

The round man nearly attached to her elbow could've been her father by the look he gave her, and she disappeared behind a curtain before I'd done more than open my mouth. "My apologies," he said, and I sidestepped his attempt to grasp my forearm.

I'd been here before—twenty years ago, not that the man recognized me now—and little had changed. Master Alfred and his three brothers grew fatter on crowns and notches earned by negotiating poor deals for those willing to live by the sword.

"The Guild currently does not have any jobs available."

Master Alfred's frown deepened when I smiled. "The line of mercs outside at that new postin' says otherwise."

"Well, yes. There are those jobs, but it would not be appropriate for a...woman," he said.

"And why not?"

His gaze followed along the adornment that curled around my leather armor before finally resting on my polished sword. "A woman of your...age might be better suited to work in a castle or large manor rather than on the dangerous road."

My cheeks grew warm, but I bit my tongue, choosing instead to fetch the scrap of parchment I carried bearin' the Guild's crest. He recognized my mercenary name as his green eyes popped against his face's sudden flush, then his eyes noted the *sepier* star pinned near my collar bone. "Lady Ida, it's been a long time since you've visited the Guild. Far too long! I meant you no slight, only...."

"Only?"

"Last job you had, you abandoned. Word was you left for a comfortable palace job, and well, the Guild has a reputation to uphold."

While tossing his ample rear across the room was my preference, I forced myself to smile. "Course ya do. But I'm not here about—"

He leaned close and whispered, "Besides, have you heard of the Merc Meister? It's not safe for women fighters—not in Loughrie anyway. My apologies, but I have nothing for you. Maybe you can check in one of the larger cities or Alesta itself."

It wasn't good enough. I wasn't leaving 'til I had a clear path to tread. "Tell me more about these murderers," I said.

His stiffened posture shifted as his hands thrust forward. Perhaps I'd gotten soft as a *sepier* or perhaps it was my old age. Either way, he'd shoved me out the door before I'd finished speaking. When the door closed in my face, I turned to find a line full of men shuffling their feet as they suppressed laughter. If I couldn't get answers from him, I'd get 'em elsewhere. "The nerve of him," I muttered, only halfway an act. Fools had no idea the dangers of being a *sepier*. All they saw was an old woman who'd gained a boon from the King. "As if I were some common merc. Damn fool."

I shoved my way through the crowd to stop before the board where I pretended to study it. Ten minutes in, someone slipped some parchment into the palm I held against my back. I didn't open it 'til I wandered away. Another ten minutes saw me tucked into the west corner table at a tavern called *The Drunken Footman* while I waited on whoever had taken my bait.

Shortly after sundown, a young man with shoulders nearly as broad as the table claimed the seat across from me. He inclined his bushy red beard in the direction of my almost empty cup, and I shook my head. His gaze flitted around the tavern while the din carried on around us. "Lady Ida hasn't visited Loughrie in over a decade. One might wonder what brings her out of her cushy retirement now," he murmured.

"Maybe she needs a little coin, is all."

Laughter erupted from the bar, and he glanced over his shoulder at a man attempting to juggle mugs while hopping from one leg to another. "Or maybe it's the Merc Meister," he said, and I shrugged. "What have you heard?"

"Four victims, all women. All died the same way."

When I didn't elaborate, he said, "Actually, there've been five victims so far. Guild only knows of four because the other one wasn't a merc." At my raised brow he added, "Commoner. Maybe she saw something."

It was plausible. If all of 'em had been mercs, that'd explain why the

Guild covered their burning. And why it was set on keeping word quiet. "Why only women?" I asked.

"No one's sure...though I have some ideas." He pointed to my throat. "The way you fled the Guild for a King is a famous tale around here. So's that scar of yours. Though no one knows how you got it. I heard some Amaskan in Sadai gave it to you."

Bile tickled the back of my throat as my muscles tensed. Who was he to know so much?

*Blue eyes, twin to my own, stared down at me. His dagger was against my throat as he laughed. "Leave? No one leaves the Order of Amaska. Not even you, sister dear. No one leaves...not alive anyway." The pinprick, then a sting as sharp as my sword slit my neck from ear to ear.*

"Lady Ida?"

I opened my eyes to find the merc's hand shaking me. "Sorry," I muttered and downed the last swallow of ale. My gaze sought his jawline, but no tattoo marked it. "Where'd ya hear this?"

"Around. People talk if you pay. If you did get that scar from them, I don't blame you for being afraid. Amaskans are born to kill. They may think they're doing holy work by killing sinners, but my Da always said, 'Bad depends on your point of view.' Nothing but rotten assassins, they are."

I nodded, but settled my hands in my lap to hide their trembling. "Why bring up my scar?"

"I think it's connected. This murderer's trying to find you. Think about it—all women with dark hair, mostly fighters, and all with their throats slit. Until I saw you outside the Guild today, I hadn't made the connection."

I swore under my breath. How many others were making the same connection? I asked, "How do I know ya aren't the killer yourself?"

"You don't. Folks figure it's a merc though. The killer seems to know where we gather, how we move, and the weapons we use." He traced circles across the tabletop with his finger as he spoke. "Details like someone's been studying mercs for a while now. But if I was the killer, I'd have just killed you rather than meet with you."

A little laugh escaped me, and he smiled—a grin made more earnest by the way his bushy, red beard danced. Something about it felt familiar, though I couldn't place it. "Have we met before?" I asked.

"I'd have remembered the honor of meeting the great Lady Ida. It's not something I'd forget."

I flushed, though whether it'd been a compliment or insult, I couldn't tell. The tavern door opened to allow entrance to a disheveled man in a black cloak. A few called out greetings as he folded his tall frame into a chair at the bar's end. His hood shadowed all but a scruffy beard and lips that trembled.

"That's Marc Silversmith," the merc said, and I glanced at the bar a second time.

Last time I'd seen Marc, he'd been one of the wealthiest caravan guards this side of the mountains. He carried the right bumps and lumps to be well-armed, but the way he'd moved through the door had been like a man with one foot in this world and the other in the next.

"Now *he's* the man you want to chat with."

"And why's that?" I asked.

"The first victim was his sister."

By the time I'd fetched another cup of ale, my informant had fled, leaving me alone with a stomach full of squirming vipers and the need of a few more cups to settle 'em. Rather than wallow in my fear, I elbowed the juggler out of his seat beside Marc Silversmith. It hadn't been all that hard considering the mixed scent of sour ale and sweat coming off my old friend. I breathed through my mouth and said, "It's been a long time, Marc."

At first, he didn't move—he kept his gaze on the bit of ale that ran down the side of his cup—but the moment I swiveled toward him, Marc fumbled for the bulge at his hip. My hand reached his dirk first, which I pressed deeper into its scabbard.

"Easy," I whispered into his ear. "It's Ida. Remember me?"

His brows furrowed as he blinked, and like someone clearing away sleep, his gaze focused on my face. "Lady Ida?" His hand went limp against mine. "You can le-go. Surprised me is all."

I released his dirk and waited another heartbeat before sliding into my seat. "I'm sorry about your sister, Dorine," I said.

"Yeah, ain't everyone."

"Can I ask ya about...what happened?" When he reached for his cup, I slid it out of reach. "You've had enough, friend. Answer a few questions for me, and I'll let ya get back to it."

"Always were a royal pain," he said with a sad little smile. "Don't know what good it'll do, but ask away."

"Where was she before the attack?"

Marc swung his arm wide. "Here. Where she always is...was. Working the bar."

"Were ya here?" Those soft, brown ovals hardened at the question, and I asked, "Did she leave with anyone? Say anythin' off or unusual?"

"No. Wish she had."

"Was she friends with any mercs in town?"

"All of them. Since you left, all she ever wanted to be was a merc like you. Even after..."

I winced, and when I pushed the cup back at Marc, he drank like a man trapped in the swirling sands of Sadai. I set a few coins on the bar before leaving him to it. What little conversation there was lulled as I passed.

Loughrie wasn't the merc's town I remembered. Not anymore.

THE POUNDING ON MY DOOR LASTED A FEW GOOD MINUTES after I'd opened my eyes and another two minutes past my shout to go away.

"Please, there's been another death," the innkeeper shouted.

Red-beard had me spooked, and I'd been all set to leave Loughrie in the past where it belonged, but another dead woman? I dragged myself out of the sad excuse for a bed with a sigh.

"Be down in a moment," I said before pulling on a linen shirt and breeches. I stuffed my feet into my boots, buckled myself into my leather armor, and was down the tavern stairs at a pace that left my old joints complaining. A man wearing the King's Army uniform chatted with the inn keep, the latter of which shoved a cup of ale and small plate of food in my direction. "I hear we have another body?" I asked and bit off a chunk of cheese.

"Lieutenant Colby," the man in blue said as he nodded at me. "Word is I'm supposed to report...to you?"

So this was the lieutenant who'd sent word to the King. "Thanks for the reports on the victims. They were quite helpful." As helpful as too much ale the night before.

"I was expecting someone—"

I slid the coin from my pouch and held it up to stop him talking. If he'd finished that sentence, I might've had to kill him. Etched into the coin was a silver star marking me as *sepier*. When he opened his mouth, I shook my head to silence him.

"Um, yes, if you'll follow me," he said.

At least this fool knew who and what I was. I trailed along as he led me out of the inn and towards a lean-to held together by little more than luck and a prayer. Inside, a soldier with a lantern stood guard over a body. When the lantern light reflected off his face, I closed my eyes. Marc's disheveled black cloak was gathered around him like a shroud, but his throat wasn't slit. The place reeked of sour wine, and a quick glance around left me wondering when he'd last been home as a layer of dust coated everything. "When was he found?" I asked.

"Landlord was around this morning to collect rent. Found him passed out. Thought him drunk until he turned him over. You think it's related to the others?" the lieutenant asked.

I ignored him as I searched Marc's pockets. His registration with the Guild was wadded up in his pants pocket along with a lock of hair. Probably his sister's. I set both aside and checked the pouch at his waist. A few coins but nothing else. I nudged his head with my boot. "Bring the lantern here," I said as I leaned closer. Something discolored his jaw near the ear, and I grabbed the throwing knife from the top of my boot.

"What are you doing?" the lieutenant hissed, and I brushed aside his outstretched hand.

"There's somethin' on his jaw." I held his beard hair taut and gently pulled the knife-edge across the hairs, cutting 'em a bit to get a better look at his skin. My insides shook as the hair fell away.

It wasn't the Amaskan tattoo I'd been dreading, but it *was* an intentional mark all the same. Someone had scratched three slanted lines into his skin.

"Looks like he scratched himse—"

My glare silenced the lieutenant. "The marks are evenly spaced and even in length. No one scratches themselves that cleanly. It's recent, too."

"Then what's it mean?"

I shook my head. No need to tell him. There wasn't anything he could do to stop what was coming or what was already here. Only an Amaskan would use that symbol. Marc had been spotted talking to me, and they'd silenced him—marked him an oath-breaker. He wasn't one, but it was a symbol I'd recognize. One meant to silence me.

The red-bearded merc had been right. The Amaskans *were* here, and from the looks of it, they were looking for me. My hands trembled as I returned my knife to its sheath.

"Burn the body immediately. Tell anyone who asks that Marc drank himself to death."

The lieutenant saluted me as I left the lean-to, my steps a lot less sure than they'd been before. It'd been twenty-five years since my brother'd left me for dead. Why would Bredych choose now to hunt for a woman believed to be dead?

I rubbed my jaw. The puffy scar marred it, but if I pressed against it, the tattoo was still there under the scar tissue. Like a curse.

A light drizzle left the morning chilly and gray as I set out for the Merc's Guild. Somewhere in this town was a red-bearded man who'd asked all the right questions. Maybe he knew more than he was letting on. Either way, I needed to find him before anyone else died.

Or before he did.

SEVERAL HOURS AND A PARCHED THROAT LATER, THE RED-bearded merc was nowhere to be found, though I'd had several folks tell me he'd last been seen at the tavern in the company of some lady merc. As afternoon rolled in with a storm, I settled into the tavern's back corner with a glass of wine and a hearty meal, though I only picked at it. Once done torturing myself with the idea of food, I tossed up my cloak's hood and retreated to the shadows.

When he walked into the tavern, Red-Beard glanced around at the dozen occupants before settling at the bar. Every time the door opened, his fingers squeezed his mug, but he otherwise kept his gaze straight ahead. A candlemark passed before he gave up waiting for me, assuming that was his goal, and left. I followed a few heartbeats behind and winced when I opened the door to the downpour.

The rain would disguise the sound of my footfalls, but it'd be harder to track him in all the shadows, which he hugged like a mistress. I used an empty wagon to reach the tavern's roof and ignored the groan in my right hip as the old injury reminded me how young I wasn't. Jumpy as Red-Beard was, I needed every advantage, and lucky for me, the buildings in Loughrie stood close together.

He was good, but not *that* good. Which meant he couldn't be Amaskan. Or if he was, he'd have to be new. Like the rest of Loughrie, he'd underestimated me, and I grinned as I followed along from the rooftops. While he meandered in the rain for a few minutes, he eventually circled around to the road leading out of town. I used the shutters on a house to climb down, careful of where I placed my feet when I landed. A light flickered in a barn up ahead as the door opened, and he stepped inside.

I spent the next few minutes dodging puddles as I prayed to the Thirteen that the storm would hide my approach. The barn was a smart choice—no real windows and two doors, three if ya counted the hay door in the rafters. My hip ached as I peered up at the hay door. It was reachable with some inventive maneuvering though I'd pay for it in the morning.

Thunder rolled overhead, and I used the opportunity to walk around the barn's side. The wood siding was too slick to scale in the rain, but luck was with me. In the rear, a ladder leaned against the barn. Perfect.

A moment later, I'd climbed in through the open hay door and sat dripping in the rafters. Below me, three voices, including Red-Beard, murmured, and I crept forward 'til I'd reached the railing. Two of the men sprawled across haystacks while Red-Beard approached. "She wasn't there," he said.

"Do you think she's onto you?"

The man who asked this slid forward off the hay, giving me a good look at his clothing. Black from head-to-toe, the fabric was fitted at the joints and waist, yet stretchable elsewhere. Cloth shoes covered his feet and when his hood fell back, his bald head shined in the lantern light.

Amaskan.

I didn't need the tattoo to confirm it, though I caught sight of the circle on his clean jaw when he turned his head my way. I held my breath, but the darkness hid me.

The face was older, the lines and wrinkles deeper, but it was the scar across his nose that confirmed it. The man pacing before Red-Beard was none other than Ilan, my brother's second-in-command. He'd been like a brother to me growing up in the Order of Amaska, and bile burned the back of my throat.

Watching him, the urge to flee was overwhelming. It'd be what he'd expect too. Always playing it safe—that was how he probably remembered me.

Red-Beard flinched as Ilan leaned close and whispered something in his ear. Red-Beard nodded, then left the barn. Fleeing was exactly my plan, but Ilan chose that moment to look up into the rafters. Behind me, the open hay-door swung in the wind and tapped against the siding.

"Got to close that door. Storm's getting worse," he said to the other guy, who shrugged in response.

I crept back as slowly as I dared and didn't turn around 'til my feet touched the ground outside. Long after I'd dried off in the warmth of the tavern, my body shivered and my skin crawled. I could've sworn his eyes still watched me. I took a long swallow of ale and waited for Red-Beard's return.

DESPERATION USUALLY DROVE PEOPLE TO STUPIDITY, BUT also to the familiar, and Red-Beard was no exception. Not long after I'd nursed my third glass of wine, he stumbled into the tavern, his cheeks flushed and his beard a dripping mess. When he spotted me, he grinned and made straight for my corner. "I've been looking for you," he said, and I nodded to the empty chair in front of me.

"We seem to have spent most the day looking for each other then."

He frowned at this. "Seems odd we couldn't find one another in a town this small, but we've found each other now. I have a proposal for you."

"Indeed? A job?"

"I...I know you've been looking into the murders, but I could see it in your eyes last time we talked."

"And what did ya see?"

"Fear. When I mentioned the Amaskans, you froze. Maybe you need a good job to forget the past. My employer's looking for those who're good at talking to people. He's looking to set up his business here in Loughrie, but the townsfolk might not be keen on the competition."

"What's he do? Your employer?" I asked.

Red-Beard pointed at my glass. "In Sadai he runs a very successful vineyard, but he's looking to expand here as the weather's more hospitable to growing grapes."

I took a sip of wine to cover my laughter. The Amaskans used both horses and wine to fund the Order. Whether he knew it or not, he'd tipped his hand with that story.

"If I decide to take your employer up on this offer, what'd I be doin'? Guardin' the wine?"

"Some, though mostly just making sure the good people of Loughrie let him make his wine in peace. Maybe some negotiating with the locals."

The tavern door opened and Red-Beard's friend, a tall man whose name I hadn't deciphered, walked in. His hood covered his bald head, but it didn't matter. From the way he slid through the space to his awareness of everyone in the room, his very movement screamed Amaskan. He tucked himself into a table alone, but his eyes flickered once in our direction.

"I'm interested, though I need to let the Guild know I've found work." While Red-Beard pretended to think it over, I studied his face. Only a few inches long, the red, wet locks of his beard curled around his face, almost hiding the tattoo on his jaw below his ear. Dry, the beard had covered the tattoo completely, but now, the barest hint of a circle was there if I stared hard enough. Three Amaskans in town wasn't a coincidence. When he nodded agreement, I said, "I can meet your employer in the mornin'. Does he already have a spot in mind, or would ya like to meet here? Usual table?"

"You know the old barn at the edge of town? Has a big tree out front?"

"Used to be a sheep farm, right?"

Red-Beard nodded. "Now it's a vineyard. Or it will be come this time next year. Locals aren't too pleased with him for buying the land, so that's where you come in. We can meet there around noon."

"Noon sounds fine. Say, never did catch your name. I figure if we're goin' to be workin' together, I might want to call ya somethin' other than 'Red-Beard.'"

He laughed and held out his arm, which I grasped by the forearm and shook. "The name's Morei," he said.

"Nice to meet ya, Morei. I'll be seein' ya tomorrow then." Or sooner if all goes well.

I stood up first and left the tavern knowing full well that both Amaskans watched me. Once outside, the downpour continued, and I sighed as I rounded the corner to the alley. I grabbed a few rocks, which I tucked into my pouch, then grabbed a handful of mud. I smeared the thick stuff across my face 'til it was mostly covered. With hope, between the darkness and mud I'd blend into the shadows. I climbed into an empty wagon, unsheathed my sword, and removed my cloak, tossing the latter over me like a tarpaulin.

It didn't take five minutes for someone to exit the tavern, and Morei stopped a few feet in front of my hiding spot. He glanced about and seeing nothing in the dim light, swore. I took one of the stones from my pouch and tossed it down the alleyway a good twenty feet away.

Morei peered into the alley as thunder rattled the buildings around us. I tossed a second stone, which bounced off a stone wall before landing in a puddle, and he stepped into the alley. I held my breath as he passed by the wagon but almost laughed aloud when a rat scurried in front of him and he flinched.

Stepping from the wagon would've made all sorts of sounds but the Thirteen must've been on my side as a bolt of lightning hit a nearby tree and set the air a-buzz. The reverberating thunder covered most of the noise. Morei spun on his heel and turned into my blade as I drove it into his gut.

"It *is* you," he muttered as he stumbled back, hand clutching his innards.

"Ya couldn't let the past stay buried any more than my brother could. I'm sorry, Red-Beard, but ya left me no choice. I wanted to run— probably should've—but I can't let 'em die for me. I'm sworn to protect these people, which I can't do if I'm dead."

Morei dropped to his knees and held out his hand. Clutched in his fingers was a silver ring. "B-belonged to Marc's sis-sister," he said. I took it from him, and he smiled. "Sorry, Lady Ida."

Damn him. I hadn't wanted to kill him. Why couldn't he have left it alone? Why join the Amaskans?

He exposed his throat. "Make it q-quick."

Before my blade moved, another blade sliced through his flesh from behind, nearly taking his head clean off. "Don't be sorry. Be Amaskan," the man muttered as he continued his forward momentum until I stood face-to-face with the third, unnamed Amaskan from the barn. He grinned and as lightning struck, he was on me, moving faster than I thought possible in the muddy mess. I brought my sword up in time to parry, but my feet slid backward in the mud. I fell to one knee, and his next blow knocked my sword from my muddy hands.

A miracle had saved me back then, but there wasn't one to save me now. His feral gaze left me shivering in the mud, and I thanked the Thirteen he wasn't my brother. If he had been, I'd already be dead.

"Ilan wanted the honor of killing the mighty Ida, King Leon's *sepier* and whore, but he'll have to forgive me this," he said.

I let him step into my space as he blathered, and I slid my fingers into my boot cuff. As thunder rattled overhead, I shoved my knife into his heart. He grunted with surprise, then fell to the ground.

The rain pelted me, washing off the mud and blood as I stood, chest heaving in the cold. My hip throbbed, the scar at my neck pricked a million pins, and my stomach churned. As much as I wanted a strong ale and good, long nap, both would have to wait. Unlike his new recruits, Ilan wasn't stupid. Too long without checking in, and he'd know something was up, so I left the bodies in the alley and set off for the barn at the town's edge.

And prayed to the gods that I wasn't about to get myself killed.

THE HAY DOOR STILL FLAPPED IN THE WIND, THOUGH A little less now that the rain was easing up. Ilan. He'd been my best friend and the first man I'd ever loved. He was family. Or had been 'til he'd held me down while my brother slit my throat.

Could I kill him as casually as I'd killed the two Amaskans in the alley?

From the rafters, I could kill him with one throw of my knives. It'd be done. And the past could stay in the past—where it belonged. King Leon never need know about who I had been or how I'd gotten my scar.

But was that the Amaskan in me talking? The killer in me? Or was I more than that now?

I shook my head, and a few pieces of hair that had escaped my thick braid in the fight stuck to my neck. The front door slid open without much effort, and Ilan grinned when I stepped inside. He held no visible weapons, but I wasn't foolish enough to think him unarmed. No Amaskan ever was.

"It's been a long time, Shendra...or should I say Ida?"

"Shendra died when her brother slit her throat," I said. His authentic smile caught me off guard, and I asked, "Does he know?"

"Who?"

"Bredych."

"Aren't you curious how I found you?" he asked as he pulled out a piece of parchment bearing King Leon's seal. "It was a beautiful thing. A King choosing his lover for his *sepier*. A woman who'd saved so many at the Little War of Three only to rise through the ranks to Captain of the Royal Guard. It's unusual for a woman to make it that far, so when the rumors reached me, I was curious, as I'm sure you understand. And my plan worked! Kill a few women, and you come running. You never were good at staying dead."

*He* was curious. *He* killed the women. Not my brother, Bredych.

I rushed him, sword before me. It was a risky move—one knife and he could end me—but he'd be expecting me to play it safe. To be the same Shendra he'd known before.

And he'd be wrong.

He was still talking when my sword plunged into him. Ilan's eyes widened as his mouth moved soundlessly for a moment. "Ya always had to gloat, didn't ya?" I said as he dropped off my blade and fell into the hay.

Unlike Red-Beard, there was no apology. No remorse to make his death easier to bear. Just the same smirk he'd worn when he'd held me down and betrayed me twenty-five years ago.

"Itova be merciful," I whispered as I closed his eyes. "But not *that* merciful."

Five murdered women had forced me to face my past. What would these three dead Amaskans do to me?

My hip, which had stopped aching somewhere in the fight, reminded me that for the moment, I was alive. I left the barn and walked into the night.

And into my future, whatever that would be.

About "Alive"

Originally published in *Swords, Sorcery, & Self-Rescuing Damsels* (Clockwork Dragon Press), "Alive" was the first short story I wrote about the side character, Ida, from *Amaskan's Blood*. Readers begged me to tell her origin story and while this isn't that story, this one gave some hints as to what she was and where she came from.

# LEARNING TO FLY

The dresses piled in the corner did little to settle the flutter in my stomach. Silly though it was, the pressure to find the *right* dress had given me nightmares in the weeks leading up to my appointment. Now that I was here, I pursed my lips together as the assistant brought out yet another gown.

"How about tryin' on this one? Look at the flare at the bottom? Sort of a mix between a mermaid dress and a fitted style?"

After a dozen dresses, all that white bled together, blinding me like a snow field until all I wanted was to hide in a blanket fort like I was five again.

Someone knocked on the dressing room door, and my stepmother poked her blond head inside. "Are we close yet, Amelia? Your father's growing tired."

The other shoe had dropped. My father. My ailing father who might only live to see me in this dress provided I could find one *today*. "We're close. I can feel it."

I lied, and the assistant scrambled through the rack of dresses along the one wall lacking mirrors.

Once the door closed, I sank into the chair behind me and rested my face between my hands. "We're not anywhere near close. My father's gonna die before I find a dress, let alone get married."

Ruby, the assistant, wrapped her wrinkled arms about my shoulders. "Honey, your—" the word was slurred with a touch of Southern drawl, "—mother had no right to place that kinda pressure on you. Whether or not your daddy dies has nothin' to do with today. This is *your* day, and we're gonna do whatever it takes to help you find that perfect dress. We're not *that* limited in our plus-size gowns that we're gonna fail. We want that dress to sing when you put it on, you hear? Now dry your eyes, and let's try on another one."

"She's not my mother," I said as I blotted my eyes with the offered tissue. "She's my stepmother, and she's evil incarnate."

The momentary laughter helped me relax, though it didn't magically transform the experience into the perfect day every bride dreamed about. Nothing would.

Taking off the dress was easy. Getting into it? A struggle of epic proportions involving wriggling my body into one mess of boning, ruffles, and too much chiffon. When Ruby tightened the laces with both hands and a foot, my head spun from a distinct lack of air.

At least this one fit. When Ruby had tried to tug the last dress over my hips, the seams had popped. Dress on, I sidled breathlessly outside. My stepmother's pained smile made the dress a no, but the way my daddy's lips drooped at the sides meant it didn't matter. It was time to go.

Before I could return to the dressing room, my daddy stood, and with shaking hands, pointed at a dress hanging alone on the rack beside him. "One last dress, honey. Why don't you give this one a go?"

He was more exhausted than I was, yet here he offered me support like always. I smiled. One more dress. For him.

Ruby trailed behind me. "Just so you know, this is a Clinestein *custom* gown."

My mouth fell open. "We can't afford that."

Ruby removed the dress from the hanger. "Don't you worry a tick about the cost. If it's *the* gown, your daddy will pay the price."

"It looks awful small..."

"These gowns are like magic. It's why folks travel from all over to have an appointment with us. We're the best for a reason."

"I'll try it. For Daddy."

I didn't have to shimmy quite so much to slip into it. The inner-liner slid across my skin like silk, and when Ruby laced up the back, it both cinched in my ample waist *and* allowed me to breathe. Like some sort of magic from a fairytale. I turned towards the mirror, and my hands shook as they lay at my sides. "I'm...it's beautiful."

From the sweetheart neckline embellished with small pearls and the embroidery that swept down the full-tulle skirt, to the actual feathers at the tulle's edge, the dress accentuated my curves without making me feel like my normal fat self. "I could fly in this. All the way to heaven."

The assistant snickered a bit behind the hand over her mouth.

"Well I could! Don't you dare laugh at me."

My momma, God rest her soul, would've shouted at me six ways to Sunday for that rude remark, and I closed my eyes a moment before forcing a smile. "I'm sorry. I shouldn't have snapped at you."

"I shouldn't have laughed. It's just you're so darlin', and I couldn't help it. Flyin' to heaven. Let's start by flyin' out to the folks, shall we?"

When the dressing room door opened, my daddy's haggard face lit like a summer firefly, and he stood as I walked toward the dais. My stepmother lifted up a piece of tulle. "Feathers? What are you, a chicken? Are you getting married or joining a circus?" she said with a short laugh.

"Ma'am, I'm gonna ask you to stop that right now. Let the young lady enjoy her day," Ruby said, her voice calm but firm.

My stepmother reached out to touch another piece of tulle, and I swatted her hand away. "What do *you* think, Daddy?"

Tears welled in his eyes as he smiled. "You look beautiful. Riley's a lucky man."

He was. I still couldn't believe I was getting married, but rather than the typical flood of happiness that should've filled me, my heart warred with my brain. I was getting married, but likely without my daddy by my side.

When I reached out to hug him, he whispered in my ear, "Look, it has pockets." His shaking fingers gave them a little tug.

Digging my fingers inside them, I returned to the wall-length mirror. Taking care of my daddy left me with little energy by day's end, yet the dress gave me life. It added color to my face and arms, and for once, my frame felt normal rather than *plus*.

I'd always been more than normal. Extra. Especially after my momma's death when I'd been ten. Between my exuberant personality and my size, nothing I did was good enough for my stepmother. But this time, my extra was everything I wanted and needed it to be. Even my boring brown eyes sparkled with...happiness? Joy?

Whatever it was, it looked good on me.

Ruby returned to the dressing room where she gathered up the cast off dresses. My daddy cleared his throat a few times, and Ruby poked her head outside of the room. "Oh, Lord. What'd I do? I'd forget my brain if it weren't attached."

He pointed at me. "Ain't ya gonna ask her?"

The woman's face brightened. "Oh my! I nearly forgot!" She turned my direction. "Are you down for this gown, girl?"

She'd asked it. *The* question. Well, the other question that was. I grinned. "Yes! I'm down for this gown!"

"Get it, girl!" said Ruby as she gave my daddy a high-five.

As I passed by my stepmother, she muttered, "I'm glad you found something that works with your...figure."

That woman could throw shade all she wanted. Today was the day I found my dress. Once behind closed doors, I asked Ruby, "If you'd be so kind?"

Ruby's subtle and gentle hands unwove the back lacings quick as a jackrabbit. When I stepped out of the gown, the world felt different, almost heavier. She returned the dress to its hanger, and I gave it another look. It really did appear smaller than it was. Not only had I fit, but I'd fit perfectly...into a dress with pockets! Nothing was more perfect!

Pulling on my jeans didn't feel as wonderful as the dress had been, and I sighed.

"It's never the same gettin' back into normal clothes, is it?"

I shook my head as I shoved my arms through my shirt sleeves. Once dressed, my hands trembled as I touched my dress. "I...I guess I just take this with me?"

"Your gonna leave it here darlin'. It's been paid for, so we'll make some adjustments and have it ready for you before the big day."

"Thanks for your help, Ruby. The dress is perfect."

The assistant smoothed out the dress on the rack. "It's to die for."

At first, I wasn't sure the woman had really said it, but when I glanced back, she wore an odd, knowing grin. *If my momma were still alive, she'd be crossing herself up one side and down the other at this woman.*

Outside, my father sat in his wheelchair, all previous evidence of his energy washed out by the gray pallor of his face as he hunched over. My stepmother tapped her phone. "Are we done here? We need to get your father home."

"Daddy, when did you pay for this dress? How'd you know it would be the one?"

His eyelids slid up as he craned his head to look at me. "Knew when I saw it. Haven't I always said I've got a magic mind?"

"But it's a custom piece. Can we really afford it?"

My stepmother's eyes narrowed. "You paid for a custom dress? Are you mad, Harrold?"

"I know what I'm doing, Cecile, now let it be."

"But—"

Their arguing wasn't new, nor was it good for Daddy's health as his hands gripped the sides of his wheelchair. Doing what I normally do, I stepped between them. "Stop yelling at my daddy. The doctor said it ain't good for his heart."

Something shifted behind me, and my stepmother's eyes widened. When I turned, my daddy was sliding from his wheelchair, and I reached out to catch him by the shoulders. His eyes fluttered, and I yelled, "Call 9-1-1!"

My daddy mouthed something soundlessly, his fingers still tangled in my brown locks as he tried to pull me closer.

With his mouth beside my ear, he whispered, "Love you, 'Melia."

Brown eyes like mine watched me for a moment, then his eyelids flickered and closed.

"No, no, no! Daddy, wake up! Stay with us. Help's coming."

I pressed my fingers against his neck, but no heart pulsed beneath his skin, and when I leaned near his mouth, not even a wheeze passed between his blue-tinted lips. In the moment, I recalled something about heart compressions and breathing from high school health class, but that had been three years ago. The details were fuzzy.

What if I broke his ribs? He was frail enough already...

My stepmother remained useless as ever, and with no one to tell me what to do, I wrapped my arms around my daddy and waited.

When the paramedics arrived, his still warm fingers remained tangled in my curls until one of them separated us. A narrow tunnel enveloped him as they began CPR, and I tried to focus on their actions as my vision grew fuzzy around the edges. If he collapsed again, I'd need to know what to do. The tunnel shrank, and my heart raced.

Somewhere off to the side, the occasional sniff and sob punctuated the orchestra of chest compressions and puffs of air. A few minutes later, one of the EMT's declared him dead, and I frowned. What did he mean dead? My daddy was a fighter!

The sympathy in the EMT's eyes was too much. I burst into tears. "He can't be gone. Not yet! I..."

Darkness hovered at the edges of my vision. I was falling, though part of me floated above the chaos. While the EMT's covered my daddy's body, a few disconnected hands and faces hovered over me in odd pockets of light.

Something sharp and foul hovered beneath my nose, and my vision traveled back at warp speed. I sat up abruptly, and an EMT pressed a hand against my chest. "Lie back down for a moment, please," he said.

"I wasn't aware I was lying down in the first place."

He watched the heartbeat monitor on my index finger while a cuff around my arm measured my blood pressure. Convinced I was breathing and otherwise normal, he removed the monitors. "She fainted," he said to my stepmother, who waved her hand.

"She'll be fine. What about my husband? Why are they covering him up?"

My lips trembled. "Cecile, he-he's gone."

She shook her head. "That wasn't the plan. He promised to outlive me!" My stepmother's legs collapsed beneath her, and the EMT's rushed to seat her into an empty chair.

Ruby, who'd been hovering nearby, handed us both glasses of water. I set mine aside to help Cecile sip a few mouthfuls.

"What will I do without him, Amelia?"

The plaintive cry sent a chill through me, and I wrapped my stepmother in a hug—the first time I'd ever been allowed to touch the woman by choice. Cecile's frail grip on me didn't feel as strong as it should've, certainly not for a woman in her early fifties, and I said a silent prayer that my stepmother wouldn't follow my daddy anytime soon.

I didn't like the woman much, but it didn't mean I wished her ill. My momma had taught me better than that. My heart fluttered off-beat. *Oh, Momma! I hope you and Daddy are together now. I miss you!*

I held my stepmother until the coroner arrived. I held her tightly and prayed.

IT WAS RAINING THE DAY WE BURIED MY DADDY. I FIGURED IT would also rain the day I married Riley, but instead, the heavens gave us the weather people pray for: 75 degrees and sunny with a gentle breeze. Just enough to give us a hint of of the Gulf Coast. Saltwater and margaritas was her bridesmaid's wedding slogan.

Despite the sun streaming through the church's open windows, in the bridal suite it was mostly cloudy with a ninety percent chance of showers. Or it would've been if my bridesmaid, Jekela, wasn't distracting me.

It wasn't that I didn't want to marry Riley—I did—but a shadow clung to my shoulders in the shape of my daddy.

There was no one to walk me down the aisle to Riley but me, and I had never been alone before.

Like a puppet, I moved where they wanted me. First this chair, where a woman with skilled hands braided my long curls until I resembled a magical princess, and then another chair where my good friend, Devon, painted my face until I looked alive and beautiful.

"Now don't you go crying and messing up all this makeup, girl! I've spent much too long on it to have it ruined. You need to cry? You better suck it in 'til you're Zen," he said as he sparkled a light dusting of glitter across my cheeks and collar bones.

The flowers arrived, and I was maneuvered into a more comfortable chair where the hair stylist wove some lilies *(Daddy's favorite)* into my braids, and Devon added more glitter. Always with the glitter, Devon was.

"You need something borrowed and something blue," said Jekela as she pulled an embroidered, blue lily from her pocket and pinned it in my hair. "This was my mother's. I'm sure she'd be honored to know you wore it. Lord knows I ain't ever getting married again, and someone should use it!"

The bridal suite door creaked open, and my stepmother poked her head inside. "May I come in?"

Jekela glanced at me, her cocked eyebrows clearly saying it was my call.

"Come in," I said.

She walked over to where I sat and held out her hand. In it was a small box older than I was, its wrapping all wrinkled and smudged with soot.

"What is it?"

Cecile shook her head. "I don't know. It wasn't mine."

"Whose was it?" I asked, but glancing at it a second time, my stomach tightened. I knew the answer.

Throughout my childhood, every household move, my daddy had packed a small box of belongings he kept out of my reach, at least until I was tall enough to peek inside when he wasn't looking. He had never allowed me to touch the box, let alone open it.

Before that, hazy memories haunted me like shadowy nightmares of the night my momma died: the fire's heat, standing outside in the pouring rain while sirens blared in the distance, and the thick smoke that permeated what remained of the house afterwards.

So strong was the memory that I almost dropped the box. Instead, I gripped it harder as my hands trembled. When I met my stepmother's gaze, she nodded the tiniest bit.

The box had been my momma's.

I brought the box up to my nose. Burnt wood and melted plastic.

The small hint of fragrance she used to wear—like coconuts and pineapple. She'd loved the tropical scents.

"She always wanted to go to Hawaii," I whispered as tears welled up in my eyes.

"No tears! I forbid it!" Devon cried as he ran up with a tissue. He dabbed as I blinked rapidly. When he turned to my stepmother, Devon jabbed a finger at her. "You're leaving now. Anyone who makes her cry gets to wait outside in the chapel."

Cecile nodded once and retreated, leaving me with the box.

"You gonna open it?" asked Jekela.

Devon shook his head. "Not if it's gonna make her cry. Is it gonna make you cry?"

I shrugged. "I don't know. It belonged to my momma."

"Oh, Lord! Mommas and weddings equal tears, but since your momma's dead, Imma let you go on. Don't make me have to redo all this makeup though. Not unless you wanna delay your wedding."

For all Devon's sass, his eyes teared up as he watched. He and Jekela were reminders that I wasn't completely alone today, and I smiled as I removed the box's lid. A thin layer of cotton lay on top, and I removed it with shaking hands.

Beneath it was a tiny vial half full of amber liquid. I picked it up and held it between my fingers. When I unscrewed the cap, the familiar smell of coconuts and pineapples wafted out, and for a moment, I was five years old again and standing in my parents' bedroom. My mother stood in front of her mirror as she dabbed perfume on both wrists and her neck.

I dabbed a small amount on my wrists before placing the cap back on the vial.

"That's an odd scent for a perfume," said Jekela.

"Momma used to pretend she was flying away to Hawaii when she took the train into town. This was her 'souvenir' from her adventures in the tropics." I blinked back tears as my sight blurred. "I haven't smelled this scent in years."

"You gonna be okay, honey?" asked Devon as he used a brush to fix my eyeliner.

I nodded as my stomach twisted. I didn't have much choice in the matter. There was only me now.

Jekela carried a large bag over to the couch. Inside rested my wedding dress, and the moment she unzipped it, my father's death threatened to bury me. That day had been a disaster with a smidge of perfect.

My bridesmaid gave my hand a squeeze. "I know this is hard, girl. Probably bringing back a ton of nightmares, but you got this. You only have to step inside, and me and Devon will do all the rest, I promise."

A puddle of feathers lay in front of my feet like a nest; I only need to step forward to fly.

I took a deep breath followed by another. My heart slowed its rapid descent into gloominess as I stepped into the smooth layers. As Jekela and Devon laced me into the gown, my hands felt useless as they dangled at my side, and instinctively, I tucked them into the gown's pockets.

For a moment, my fingers were alone inside the silk, but as I dug them in deeper, my index finger brushed against something rough.

"Hold still," said Jekela as I wriggled.

"There's something in my pocket."

Devon bunched up his nose. "Like a receipt or something? How tacky!"

"I'm not quite sure. It feels like...paper? Something paper-like." When I grasped hold of the object, it flittered away, and I dug my hand deeper into the pocket.

"Dayyum, girl! How deep those pockets go, anyway?" asked Jekela.

I stretched my fingers as far as I could. With the skirt out at my side, it was easier to see where my fingertips were. "Deep," I said.

"Your daddy always did have some deep pockets."

Jekela laughed at Devon's joke, though my eyes welled up. He'd been so proud to find a dress I could love.

"Hey now, don't cry," said Jekela as she punched Devon in the shoulder. "See what you done?"

"What I did?"

The two of them bantered back and forth as I resumed my search. I flipped the pocket inside-out, but it was empty. Just like when I'd tried it on in the dressing room at Clinestein's. On a whim, I stuck my left hand in the other pocket where my fingers brushed against crisp paper. The edge was sharp enough to sting, and when I yanked my hand out, my index finger was bleeding.

"Did you just go and get a paper cut from that damn receipt?" asked Devon. He grabbed a bandage from his kit-o'-everything and wiped my finger clean.

When he stuck his hand into my pocket, I shouted, "Hey!"

"Beautiful though you are in this dress, honey, you *know* you ain't my type." When he removed his hand, he held an off-white envelope with a single drop of blood at the edge. "Well, looky here! A pre-marriage love note from Riley? Or do you got another lover on the sly?"

"He's never seen the dress, and no, don't even jest. Maybe it's well-wishes from Clinestein's. They *are* supposed to be a full service business," I said as I held out my hand. "Either way, it's meant for me."

Devon handed over the envelope. "I guess so seeing how you even bled for it. Now don't go cutting yourself again gettin' it open."

I ran a fingernail beneath the flap. Instead of a pre-printed message from Clinestein's, the paper held my daddy's long cursive. On the outside, one word: Amelia.

Much to my chagrin, my fingers trembled as I sat down to read the letter dated today.

*Dear Amelia,*

*If you're reading this, then this cancer's taken me, and you're standing in the bridal suite getting ready for your big day. I know I promised to be there with ya, but sometimes life has other plans. Not even I can thwart the path set for me, no more than ya can avoid the one set for ya. I wanted to write this letter because I didn't want ya to feel alone.*

*I know you, my Amelia.*

*Devon's probably chided you a dozen times about ruining his beautiful makeup, while Jekela's attempting to keep ya laughing, but inside, you're grieving. You're hurting, but so is Cecile. I know ya don't like her, but she's grieving, too. Besides, she's done something very sweet for ya.*

*Your dress is beautiful. I knew it the moment I saw it, but there were a few things missing. For one, its skirts didn't feel full enough for someone full of joy like ya are, so I asked them to add more joy to the dress. Here's where your stepmother came in. She wanted ya to be comfortable and to feel like you, so she brought up the idea of pockets.*

*Thing is, she already had some.*

I put the letter down for a moment. It was hard to remember my stepmother's grief, especially when she took such pleasure in reminding me how imperfect I was. On a day I felt alone, she'd not only brought me something of Momma's, she'd also suggested something so perfectly me: pockets.

My daddy's handwriting blurred, but I continued reading.

*I didn't believe it at first. I mean, who would. But I'm getting ahead of myself.*

*Anyway, your stepmother came to me with these old pockets that looked like they'd been ripped out of her own dress. They weren't attached to anything anymore. She told me her mother had made them as part of her own wedding dress. When she'd died, the pockets were passed on to Cecile. She never did figure out exactly how it works, only that it does. See, her momma had the Touch. Some call it a blessing while others would see it as a curse. Your momma would've called it the Devil, but Cecile calls it magic.*

*Cecile's momma sewed these pockets into Cecile's dress. See, right after your stepmother married her first husband, he got sent off to fight in 'Nam. Her momma was afraid Cecile would never see him again, but with these pockets, your stepmother could keep in touch. She'd write him letters, then stick 'em in a pocket. They'd disappear, and a while later, his response would arrive. It didn't matter what pants he was wearin' neither. As long as she used the pockets of her wedding gown, she could always reach him.*

"I think my daddy might've gone crazy," I muttered, and Jekela glanced up from my shoebox.

"Well, he *was* undergoing chemo. I've heard that stuff messes with your brain a bunch."

I shook my head. "He had the time to write me a letter before he died, but all he's talking about is magic pockets."

Devon bust out laughing. "Really? You mean the ones in your dress?"

"Yeah."

"Chemo madness, I'm telling ya." Jekela held up my shoes. "You ready for these?"

"Not yet. Let me finish reading."

She waved her hand at me as she set my shoes to the side.

*I know it sounds like I've gone mad, but this isn't the chemo talking, baby girl. After your momma died, I would've given anything to talk to her or touch her again. When I married Cecile, the first time she went away for business, she showed me the pockets. She'd sewn them into her wedding gown when she'd married me. She was so pretty that day, I didn't even notice her dress had pockets at all. But that's beside the point.*

*At first, I thought I'd hit my head or had too much to drink, but no matter how many times I tested the things, they worked. Don't exactly know how, only that they do. She and I used them off and on until I got cancer, and she stopped traveling. Thing is, they only work when sewn into a wedding dress. Always a wedding dress.*

*If you ever have a child, you could sew them into her dress, and it would continue working, assuming it still has the magic. For some reason, its power's disappearing. Messages occasionally go missing, never to appear where they're supposed to. Been like that for the past three years or so.*

*But the thing is, Cecile's given you a great gift.*

*See, I may be dead, but she's been talking to me still. Giving the pockets to ya means she ain't ever gonna talk to me again. These things will only work for you now. She misses me something fierce, but she wants ya to be able to say goodbye, so she's passed them on.*

They couldn't work.

Magic didn't exist no matter how much I wanted to talk to my daddy. But if they did... If there was any possible way they worked, Cecile had sacrificed something unique and special, so that I could say a proper goodbye.

Tears rolled down my cheeks. Somewhere in the distance Devon sighed, but I ignored it as I continued reading.

*I know you're too smart to just trust me on this. I ain't been myself for a while now, so I don't blame ya for doubting, but there's a way you can find out. Take a leap of faith for me, baby girl. Just scribble a short message for me on the back of this and stick it in your pocket. If nothing happens, you've taken a moment to say goodbye, but if it does work, then you'll know.*

*Just in case—yeah, I know it works, but even I have doubts sometimes—I want ya to do something for me, honey. Live. Live a good life. Take care of Riley, and take care of you. Not many folks get to write a letter like this knowing they're gonna die, but I've been ready for a while now. Cancer don't spare folks, so... You've spent your whole life living for others. It's that servant's heart you have, but at some point, you gotta stop asking others what to do and take the lead.*

*Believe in yourself. I know ya can fly.*

*I love you,*

*Your dad.*

At some point, the mess of letters solidified again, but if I dared look at his words, they'd blur up lickety-split. "Does anyone have something to write with?" I asked, and Jekela handed me a pencil.

"Whatcha doing now? Writing back?" she asked.

"Something like that. I'm saying g-goodbye."

She wrapped her arm about my shoulders as I sobbed, feeding me tissue after tissue until I'd exhausted my tears.

Someone knocked on the door, and Devon answered it. "No, not yet. Maybe another twenty minutes. We're on schedule...mostly," he said with a glance in my direction.

While he answered another question, I scribbled out a message on my daddy's letter.

*I don't believe in magic. Not since you died.*
*I miss you, Daddy.*
*Goodbye.*

I folded the letter, tucked it into my left pocket, and waited. Two minutes passed and when nothing happened, Devon sighed and set his kit-o'-everything in the chair beside me.

"Let's fix this mess you've made of your face." He tugged a wet wipe from its package. "Again."

Most of his hard work was water resistant, but there was only so much flooding it could take, so he wiped away the glitter and colors to begin again. This time on a time crunch.

While he worked, Jekela told me jokes from the Internet to make me laugh until Devon ordered her to stop. "You're moving around too much!"

He was about finished when something pressed against my thigh. "No way," I muttered, and they both stared. "I think something's in my pocket."

"Well, yeah. You stuck the letter in there," said Jekela.

"No, my other pocket."

She tilted her head. "You sure you didn't just mess up on which pocket you stuck it in?"

"No. I made sure of it."

Devon shook his head like we were both crazy. "Well, take it out then. Let's see what kinda voodoo you done got yourself into."

At first, I waited a moment to experience the weight of it on my leg. Almost like my daddy's hand. When I tucked my fingers into the pocket, it was definitely the same piece of paper, and I removed it with a sigh. Maybe Jekela was right. Maybe I'd forgotten which pocket I'd used and nothing more.

I unfolded the letter. My father's side was the same as it had been, but when I flipped it over, there was new writing below my own.

*Ya found my letter! Thank God!*
*Ya may not believe in magic, honey, but it believes in you!*
*I miss ya, too. I betcha look beautiful today.*

My hands shook so hard I dropped the letter. When Devon picked it up, he yelled, "Holy Mary, Mother of God! There's writing on there!" He clapped his hands together. "Dear God, I'm sorry I ever doubted you existed. I'll go to church now, like my mom wants. Amen."

"You don't know it came from God. Maybe this is the Devil's work," said Jekela.

I wagged my finger at her. "Don't you ever suggest my daddy's involved in something unholy!"

When I held out my hand, Devon handed the paper to me, and I stared at it. Was it really him? I took the pencil and scribbled a note back.

*Is it really you? How are we talking? Are you in Heaven? Is Momma there? Are these pockets...of the Devil? Does this mean we can talk forever?*

It didn't take as long for the response, though it was shorter than I wanted.

*We don't have a lot of time. Like I said in the letter, these pockets have limited energy or magic or whatever it is left. I know ya have questions, but it's your big day. You've got places to be. This was only meant to give you and me a chance to say goodbye. I love ya so much. I'm so proud of who ya are and who you're gonna become.*

"That's it?"

Jekela squeezed my shoulder. "Honey, you're getting a chance no one else does. Be happy for it, not critical."

I stared at my daddy's scribbled response. There was so much more I wanted to know, *needed* to know, but he acted like we didn't have the time. "I'm trying, but why give me the power to speak to him, only to take it away? Does that make any sense to you?"

My friends remained silent as my emotions whirled enough to make me dizzy. Jekela wasn't wrong. No one else got to talk to their daddy after he died, at least not that I knew of. Why couldn't I be happy with it?

He said the pockets were limited now, but I decided to risk it.

*Daddy,*
*There's so much we never got to say or do. I wish you were here to*
*walk me down the aisle. I'll try to be the kind of woman with inner*
*strength, the kind who takes the lead and isn't angry that magic*
*existed only to say goodbye.*
*I love you so much.*

While this letter disappeared quickly, nothing reappeared. I waited and waited, but my pockets remained empty. "What if they don't work anymore?" I asked, my heart beating a furious race in my chest.

"Then, honey, at least you got to say goodbye," said Devon.

I wanted to be angry with the softness of his words, but I couldn't. Not to Devon who'd never said hello to his father, let alone goodbye.

Jekela placed my shoes in front of me. "No more stalling, honey. It's time."

She held my arms as I stepped into my slippers, and Devon rolled his eyes. "I can't believe you're wearin' those things," he said as he pointed at my house shoes.

"Hey, if I'm going to be on my feet for the next umpteen-hours, I wanna be comfortable. Besides, in this dress, no one can see my feet anyway."

Everything in place, Devon held the door open for me, and I stepped into the hallway. Jekela rushed forward to where my other bridesmaids stood, and Devon entered the chapel to take his seat.

The music inside the chapel shifted, and the line in front of me stepped forward toward the door. My stomach danced in rhythm to the beat. Inside, Riley waited for me, for us to begin our life together. For a moment, my mind ignored the music as it waited for another note.

*One last time, please?*

The procession continued their walk down the aisle, and I readied myself to follow.

Alone.

I gripped my bouquet with my right hand, and as I stepped forward, something much heavier than a note dropped into my left pocket. I shoved my hand inside, expecting to feel paper, but instead, my fingers touched skin.

My feet stumbled as I entered the chapel, and the guests murmured. Devon stood to rescue me if needed, but my flat slippers gave me enough purchase to steady myself. As my left hand touched the warm skin inside, my fingers brushed against the familiar callouses of my daddy's palm and up to his roughened fingertips. My index finger traced the familiar circle engravings on his wedding ring and the smoothness of his trimmed nails.

Ready to lead, I stepped forward and felt my daddy take my hand in his. A bright smile spilled across my face. The pocket was giving me one final gift.

My daddy was walking me down the aisle.

Unlike the rehearsal, the walk wasn't long. In fact, I could've sworn only a few moments passed between when my daddy took my hand and when he let go. I'd reached Riley, whose handsome face lit up like heaven at the sight of me. I hoped the same glow appeared in my eyes that danced in his, and as he reached out to take my hand, my daddy's disappeared.

For a moment, I reached down my pocket to find him, only the pocket had shrunk. It was time to let go.

It was time to fly.

ABOUT "LEARNING TO FLY"

I love this story. I wrote it in one sitting at the *Rainforest Writers' Retreat* in the Hoh Rainforest of Washington. Originally "Learning to Fly" was to be published in the *It Has Pockets Anthology* (Clockwork Dragon Press) but one of the editing partners died suddenly and the press fell through. If you've ever watched a certain show on *TLC* about picking out wedding gowns, you'll get a lot of the jokes in this story. This was my humoristic poke at such a show and all the bridezillas out there, but also my reminder that we all need to fly.

This story is dedicated in memory of Jeff Cook. You are missed.

# THE DRIVE TO WORK

I am up long before Pierce's alarm wakes him at 7:00 A.M., plenty of time to see him off to work by ten. Not that I have to drive him —the car drives itself these days—but he likes the company and what can I say, so do I. Besides, if I'm in the car with him, the car can use the carpool lanes, getting him to work a full hour before the rest of traffic hits downtown.

When Pierce crawls out of bed, I have a cup of coffee waiting for him along with some scrambled eggs. For twenty years, I woke up to the smell of eggs and coffee as it was Pierce who was the early-to-bed, early-to-rise type in those days, but once I went freelance, our relationship shifted. Now I'm the one who surprises him with breakfast! Yes, the coffee machine runs on a timer, and yes, the eggs are pre-scrambled and cooked by machine, but *I* place the plate and cup on the counter for him. *I* keep the cat away from both.

*I* wait for him to wake up and start his day with me.

His tenor bounces around the bathroom for his twenty minute shower before he walks into the kitchen wearing a bathrobe. Even at seventy, his less-slim-than-when-we-met frame leaves me breathless, and he smiles as he takes a sip of the black coffee.

"Is this a different roast from yesterday?" he asks, and I nod as I push the Sriracha towards him.

"Did you see the news about the new rail station?" I ask. The man loves his Sriracha, but this morning, his eggs remain a splatter of yellow against deep blue plates. I steal a bite while he's glancing at his email. "They want to raise taxes again to help pay for a northward expansion."

Pierce frowns into his coffee cup. "They just raised taxes last quarter."

Idle chit-chat flits in and out my ears. The news, the weather, and hell, even the *76 Smiths* coming to town—a group Pierce abhors, he calls out as he dresses for work.

"Where are my shoes?" Pierce shoves his keys into his jean pocket as I point to a black shoelace poking out from beneath the couch.

I gesture towards his nearly untouched coffee, but he's one arm into his jacket as he's opening the front door. "The carpool lane will get us there in plenty of time," I remind him as I abandon the plate and cup to the cat. "No need to rush."

When he kisses my forehead, time freezes for a moment, and there's just the warmth of him mixed with the sunlight that streams in the open door. He tugs my hand toward the detached garage, where he opens the door for me. Never mind that the door will open itself, it's the fact that he chooses to open it for me that makes me smile.

Two minutes later, our car zips through traffic as we chat until it reaches the 405, a triple-decker highway that runs mostly north and south through the Eastside. While I miss the leisurely action of a drive through the mountains, nothing about gridlock is worth missing, and I pat the car's dash where the computer calculates the optimal route and speed.

Our two-person vehicle—a beat-up, old hatchback we had converted to auto-driver a few days before the legal deadline—wedges its way across when an error beeps. "Every morning, I swear," I mutter as I touch the screen to override whatever complaint the car has today. "Old cars and bugs. A match made in hell."

The car gives a shudder before it accelerates until it reaches the carpool lane.

The dash reads 9:03 A.M. "We made good time," I say to Pierce as he glances again at his messages. Every year someone lobbies to change the variable carpool hours and every year, the laws remain the same. "Any earlier and we'd be paying the toll. You should have eaten your eggs or at least finished your coffee."

"Are you going to lecture me every morning on my way to work?" he asks, his lopsided grin half-hidden in the AR display in front of him.

"Are you going to read emails all the way to work?"

Pierce dismisses the screen with a hand wave and turns to face me. "What would you like to talk about this morning, and not politics. I'm so tired of thinking about politics."

Colors dance in my peripheral as the car shifts into a lower gear and changes lanes. We're leaving the carpool lane, and I frown.

"Attention vehicle DH9-0RS-B, you are in violation of Section 45.2 of the Washington State Department of Licensing Handbook. Please prepare your identification for Officer Manning," the car states as it continues to the right until it reaches the hazard lane.

"Section 45.2? That doesn't make any sense," I say to Pierce as I press my thumbprint to the car's touch screen. Information released, the car displays it across the side windshield for the Officer's view. "It's after 9 AM. We have the required number of occupants to use that lane, so why are we being pulled over?"

Pierce pats my arm. "I'm sure it's nothing. Perhaps a mix-up or something."

I take a deep breath as my insides quiver. I can't explain it, but the idea of being pulled over when I've done nothing wrong sends my body into fight or flight mode. Had our car been manually drivable, I would have been tempted to flee.

Instead, I practice breathing as I await Officer Manning. "He's making us wait," I mutter as two minutes flip by. "He had our information ages ago."

"Be patient." Pierce—always the calm one—glances back at the flashing red and blue lights behind us.

Because I am watching Pierce, I don't notice the officer at my window until I hear him tap on the glass. A small shriek escapes my lips as I roll down the window. "Good morning, Officer Manning. I think there has been some sort of mistake—"

"Mrs. Whitby, you are in violation of—"

"Section 45.2, I know," I say as I wave a hand at Pierce's protests from the seat beside me. The officer glances into the car, then returns his gaze to me and frowns. "I'm sorry for interrupting, Officer, but I don't understand why we were flagged for a violation. After 9 A.M., the law clearly states that a two-person vehicle may occupy the carpool lane without a toll, which my vehicle did upon entrance to the highway."

The officer frowns. "Mrs. Whitby, have you had anything to drink today?"

"What? No! It's barely 9 A.M. Pierce, tell him." I reach right, fumbling for Pierce's hand, and when I find it, he squeezes my fingers gently. "Officer, I don't understand what I've done wrong. I'll take a breathalyzer if that's what you want, but I'm just trying to have a ride in the car with my husband on his way to work. Just tell me what I've done wrong."

The corners of Officer Manning's mouth fall, and his eyes get that look that screams pity and patience. "Mrs. Whitby, are you aware that you are alone in the car?"

My brows furrow to refute him, but when I turn to my right, the seat beside me is empty. Pierce isn't there, and for a moment, my heart lurches out of my chest.

"Are you all right?" Officer Manning asks as he places a hand on my shoulder.

I flinch. One too many hands have encircled my shoulders this past week and the memory of each and every one of them comes roaring back like a freight train.

"We're so sorry for your loss."

"Our condolences, Helen."

"I'm so sorry, honey. Let me know if there's anything I can do."

Their words bury Pierce all over again, and I'm alone in the car. A single occupant driving in the carpool lane to a place I don't work.

"I-I'm sorry," I whisper to the officer. "My husband, I-I think...um, he died, and I guess I forgot..."

Officer Manning nods. "The car was registered in his name, Mrs. Whitby, so the computer told me. Is there someone I can call for you?"

For all that I don't want to be alone, the only person I want to be with is no longer here. My eyes stare at the empty seat beside me, and I shake my head.

"I don't think you should be alone right now," says the officer.

"I think I'll go home."

The officer cocks his head as he peers at me, then shrugs. "Make sure you go straight there. And no carpool lane," he says before he returns to his vehicle.

My car makes a slight beep as the officer releases control of it. "Please state your destination," the car says, and my heart lurches again as bile burns the back of my throat.

I don't want to go home, but I can't stay here.

I open my mouth when something gently squeezes my hand. When I glance in the seat beside me, Pierce is there. His smile brightens the car, and when the car repeats its request, I have an answer.

"Time to go to work."

ABOUT "THE DRIVE TO WORK"

Another one of my psychological stories, "The Drive to Work" was my attempt to deal with a nightmare I had about my partner dying. How would my life change or would it change at all? This is another story that came to me all in one go. That doesn't always happen, but when it does, it drops the mic.

# THE RINGERS

It was an eerie fog if ever there was one.

If fog could envelop every pore of every creature, even then it could not be as dense and adhering as it was that night.

Far outside the grand city of Veleden cowered a village of silence. Whereas you or I might expect sugarplums and mirth in the early days of winter, the village of Dekwood embraced grays and blacks as evening fell, and its people secured their windows against the creeping fog.

Children buried themselves beneath well-worn quilts, but they didn't clamp their eyes shut. No, they slapped tiny hands over their ears to ward off the jingle-jangle of horses' reins as the Ringers approached.

A guardsman leaned across the jingle-jangle bridle of his perfectly normal-looking horse as it crossed the threshold into town. Snowflakes sprinkled across his red suit and blended in with his white sash. The four men in his brigade, if they could be called men, pulled up alongside him.

Five muzzles puffed frost into the air.

Five men, skin haggard as it draped skeletal frames, sat astride the white beasts.

Five days they would ride and rid Dekwood of those unneeded, those too bold for purpose.

A lone child coughed as he huddled against a tree. Tears mingled with snot as he muffled his cries with a ragged scarf. The bells jangled, the eerie sound carrying through the eve like a death keen. The child froze like the snow beneath him, and five faces grinned.

THE DAY WE SOUGHT REFUGE IN DEKWOOD HELD NO SPECIAL purpose. Two seasons without work and my papa devised our bold plan. We would load up our belongings in a simple carriage and head north for better fortune.

I was fourteen, convinced I understood everything while understanding very little. It was a dark time to travel, but my mother's womb thickened with my brother and food grew scarce when the grand forests shriveled and died.

How does a forest die? Perhaps it was nothing more than a lack of rain or some magician's grim spell that shriveled the leaves mid-summer and rotted the bark 'til the logs fell without the help of a woodsman's axe. If logging was no longer lucrative, perhaps the more industrialized work of Dekwood could line my papa's pockets.

Five days' travel had left me without purpose. I taxed my mother's patience as I spoke of a spell to change rain into snow or the logic behind the life-giving elements that connected all living creatures and powered the magics of our world. When my feeble attempts to bring about snow froze my mother's morning tea, she hid my magical texts in a locked trunk. Their absence didn't stop me from walking beside the carriage to draw upon the soil's power. Every few hours' travel, I tugged the gloves from my fingers and spread them across the hard earth to feel the thrum of magic beneath me.

And when my mother wasn't watching, I'd whisper the words to call forth a slight dusting of snow across my brow. If she wondered why my red hair bore crystalline flecks, she remained as silent as our days on the road.

On the sixth day of travel, heavy snowflakes tickled my nose. They spread themselves across the hardened dirt road which snaked north to Veleden and south to the City of Escen. I'd never set foot in either, but

I'd heard Tellers talk of the great magistrates who managed the towns of the North.

Rumors traveled about the Magistrate of Dekwood, an ageless and grim man who ruled from a hillside mansion. People said he mourned the loss of his sons. Whether from a factory accident or illness, I refrained from asking. Such tales were for *children*.

I was no mere child. I couldn't be if I wished to study magic. One day I would be a magician--capable of powerful magics to bring the trees to bloom and the rivers to flow.

And force the clouds to snow.

I opened my mouth to inquire after Dekwood, but my mother's pursed lips left me silent. My feet ached, but watching my mother struggle to maintain her posture on the bumpy trail made me glad to be walking alongside the carriage. Papa grinned down at me from the coachman's seat.

No manor homes or farms dotted the countryside nor any indication that we grew closer to our destination. I wrinkled my nose when a snowflake graced it, and my mother sighed. "Elise, if you continue to make such expressions, you'll gain wrinkles before you're wed."

Before my soon-to-be brother, an accident that puzzled the Physics aplenty, my mother had spent her days raveling yarn at the seamstress's shop. Like a skein of yarn, wrinkles twined their way across her forehead, and I grinned. "Yours are what I love best about you."

My brashness earned me another scowl before she busied herself with her knitting.

I tried to follow the air across my mother's belly to hear the whispers of my brother--as the Physics had done when my mother had taken ill--but it was only wind to me, the magic far beyond my abilities.

"Papa," I said, and his wood-warped hands tightened on the reins. "Will Dekwood have a school? Something beyond the elementary standard? Perhaps someone with magical knowledge to prepare me for the entrance exams?"

Firm fingers loosened their grip. "Any place that close to the City of Veleden is bound to have something. You'll be back to your preparations in no time."

Day ten brought us over yet another hill. A gritty forest loomed ahead like something out of a nightmare, and I shivered beneath my woolen cloak. "Are we to travel through there?" I asked.

His skin paled as we observed the swaying tree-corpses that cast long shadows across the trail. "Don't tell your mother. Go distract her while we pass."

I peeked in the carriage's window. My mother lay across the crunchy, thin-padded seat, eyes closed and breath slow. Her pale hair was messed against a pillow. "She's sleeping." I glanced at the trees and whispered, "But let's hurry."

The whites of his eyes reflected his fear, an odd emotion in a man who scaled great heights for his trade, and I shivered.

"Agreed. Last we need is your mother carrying on about evil curses cast upon our future." My papa laid a superstitious hand upon his heart.

Winter tightened its grip on the dead oak, and their bones shivered. Even barren, the trees' branches stretched across the sky and blotted out all light. Like the shriveled fingers of the dead they drooped down and reached for us, stealing our warmth and joy before we were more than a foot into the woods.

Nothing lived in these trees.

No sound besides the muffled hoof beats in frozen snow. No smell beyond the burn of cold air in the nostrils. Branches snagged along my cloak, and I pulled it tighter across my shoulders.

I held my breath 'til I thought I might burst. When I glanced at the spot beside me, my papa did the same and I laughed. The glee bounced beyond us and reverberated back, amplified and shrill.

"Hush," he whispered.

Every now and again, the marks of a woodsmith scored the narrow tree trunks, and a hollow log lay beside our path, a fallen soldier in the battle of survival. And so we traveled for nigh two candlemarks.

Just as we broke free of the forest, my mother sneezed and startled a shrill cry from my lips. "Control yourself, Elise," she said through the carriage's open front window. "A young lady need not give in to such whimsies."

She met my gaze but her death grip on her shawl relayed how long she had been awake.

Papa tapped my shoulder.

Nestled among the countryside's hills, homes rose from the hard earth, their rooftops covered in winter and chimneys smoking with warmth. A great warehouse marred the image, as did the grim mansion on a hill. Dekwood.

Papa grinned. "Welcome home."

No one greeted us. No children scattered snow in the streets or chased a dog into alley carts. A few faces peered out dirty windows the size of dinner plates before fading into darkness.

At the village's center stood a grotesque statue of a man too tall, with a grin too wide that stretched his mouth past redemption. His horse-like teeth were carved of marble, and his hands held a skein of wool.

"Who's that?" I asked.

"The magistrate maybe?" guessed Papa. "Can't think who else would get a statue made of polished stone."

My mother tapped on the glass. "We've a place to go tonight, don't we?"

"From the magistrate. Said so in his letter."

The horses slowed before a brick monstrosity two stories high with edges of cast iron beams and cobbled bricks and stone. Not a brick out of place, and yet the dingy gray embraced the building and marred its appearance.

My mother alighted from the carriage with Papa's assistance. "What is this place?"

"Welcome to the inn," Papa said. He tied the reins to the post out front with a clove hitch.

"Surely we're not staying *here*, are we? Where will the horses be stabled? And the carriage?" My mother pouted at the imposing building, not at all to her customary taste. Inside, loosely grouped chairs and tables gathered dust. A single patron sat at the bar, completely ignoring us.

The woman behind the counter gave Papa a light smile. "You must be Erol Jankin. We've been wonderin' when you'd get here." She squeezed wide hips through the bar opening and ambled over to us, thick pink skirt ruffles dusting the floor as she moved. "The name's Beatrice."

My mother ignored the woman's offered hand, but Papa seized it with exaggerated enthusiasm. "Thanks for the welcome. Noticed quite an oddity on the trip here--that...forest "

Beatrice gave him a curt nod. "You're welcome to two rooms upstairs 'til you can get somethin' of your own. The carriage and horses outside?"

Papa nodded. "In his letter, the magistrate said he'd board the horses--sell the carriage to cover room and board."

"For you and the missus, maybe, but the rooms're too small for the three of you. You'll need another room."

My mother's mouth popped open. "We'd be indebted to this magistrate."

Beatrice's soot-colored eyes settled on the heap of books in my arms. The woman paled at the infinity symbol on the cover, and said, "Shouldn't be long before something comes available, I wager."

The lone patron excused himself as my mother voiced her complaints. Papa forced a smile as Beatrice handed him two keys. "Ain't a kitchen or anything in the rooms, but there's a restaurant 'cross the way that serves meals. I've got the usual helpin's of meat and potatoes in the evenin'. Bread and cheese in the mornin'. I lock up at midnight. If you aren't inside by then, you'll be locked out."

Papa pocketed both keys, ignoring my outstretched hand. "Thank you."

"Won't I need my key?" I asked, and my mother shushed me. "Mother, I'm fourteen. If I am old enough to attend the Academe, surely I could be trusted with my key?"

"No, ma'am." Beatrice wagged a plump finger at me. "You listen to your folks. Stay in your rooms at night, no matter what you...hear."

"What would we hear?" I asked.

"Bells."

My mother tugged me toward the stairs.

"Bells?" I asked.

"I'll send Vincent to help you unload your belongin's," said Beatrice, and Papa nodded his thanks.

Three steps from the top, I turned to face my mother. "The bells of the spirits? Is that what she meant?"

My mother pressed a finger to my lips. "Don't make trouble."

When I opened my mouth, Papa shook his head. "Listen to your mother."

I didn't know what shocked me more--that there were spirits in town or that Papa agreed with my mother. Either way, I was determined to remain awake and listen for the bells.

MORNING BROUGHT A MISTY RAIN TO DEKWOOD. WE STOOD in the town square, woolen jackets doing little to keep the chill off our shoulders. Either the bells had never sounded, or I'd fallen asleep.

A little slip of a man rushed over to us. Raindrops dripped off his umbrella and splashed upon my plaits.

"Are you Erol Jankin?" he asked, and Papa nodded. "I'm Magistrate du Leunt's assistant. The magistrate sends his most profound apologies."

"Erol, you said--"

Papa patted my mother's gloved hands, tightly knotted over her thickened waist. "I understand, Mr...?"

"Nicolas Ashton. The magistrate can hardly meet everyone who stumbles into town, no matter how...desperate their letters may appear. I'm sure you understand, Mrs. Jankin." He tipped his hat in my mother's direction.

To my father, he said, "I understand your former occupation was a logger in Devlon. I'm afraid we don't have a need for such work. If you wish to pay back your debt to the magistrate--"

"I was given to believe our carriage would cover our time at the inn," said my mother.

"Your carriage was hardly fit to cover your stay for a day, let alone a lengthier time." My mother glared at Papa.

Whatever the magistrate had arranged, our plans had changed. My mother squared her shoulders before she spoke. "Then I'm afraid we must take our leave of Dekwood."

Papa whispered something in her ear. Her face paled before her cheeks flushed like a ripe strawberry.

"As I was saying, men work in the leather mill or out in the fields with the sheep." Mr. Ashton frowned as he noted Papa's lanky figure. "I suppose you'll do with the tanner. Little old for apprenticing but work hard, and you could clear your sizeable debt in perhaps a year's time."

Sizeable? We had slumbered here one evening yet our debt was sizeable? Tuition for the Academe would stretch us beyond our means with my mother's need for society life, but surely a few seasons missed work had not brought us to such dire straits? Papa's hand rested on my shoulder, and I bit my tongue.

"Women and those not able-bodied work in the textile factory. Everyone pulls their share in Dekwood," continued Mr. Ashton.

"I'll admit to never having worked with leather before, but I figure can't be much harder than climbing trees in the nippy winter. Say, I was going to ask the magistrate about schools."

"School?"

"Yes, for Elise. Back in Devlon, she was readying for entrance into the--"

The man's nose twitched with impatience as he waved a hand at Papa. "She's too old for school here. As long as she's got the basics, she has all she needs. Doesn't take much by way of brains to work in the factory, now does it?"

"The factory? But, sir, I'm to study magic at the--"

Like a striped tomcat of Devlon, the man hissed as he stepped back. "Magic isn't tolerated or needed in Dekwood. You'll be working in the factory or none at all."

"Then I'll take none, sir, as I have studies to attend to." Papa's fingers pinched my shoulder, and I winced.

"If you know what's good for you, you'll nip that in the bloom now," Mr. Ashton said to Papa with the wag of his finger. "If you want to stay in Dekwood, these are your options." Papa nodded and Mr. Ashton continued. "Work begins an hour after sunrise. Report to the tanner's at noon, and he'll fill you in on the rest. It's just down the street a few buildings and on the right."

"What about housing?"

His eyes, thin charcoal slits at the bottom of too large a forehead, rested on me, and that grin returned. "You shouldn't be too long in the inn."

He'd made it three steps toward the mansion in the distance when Papa called out, "We'll be in contact if we need something. Thank you, and thank the magistrate."

My mother elbowed him in the ribs. "When were you going to tell me of our debt? Had I realized we'd amassed so much in Devlon--" Her cheeks flushed as she turned her eyes on me. Unusually frizzy hair popped out from beneath her wide-brimmed hat, whose red poinsettias clashed with the rich plum of her scarf. She tucked the escapee behind her ear. "Dally about in the rain if you wish, but I've no purpose in this...mess."

We trailed behind her to the inn. A wide road such as this should have played host to many, yet it remained empty. My mother tugged on the doorknob of the inn's solitary door, but the swollen wood stuck.

Papa gave it a good tug and when it released its grip, my mother had an additional reason to scowl so early in the day. The door banged shut behind her. "She'll find reason enough to smile once our situation's settled," said Papa.

I only half heard him as I studied the rain. Like the town, winter here lacked its usual patterns.

As if he'd followed my thoughts, Papa said, "I suspect everyone's at the leather mill or the textile factory. Odd little town this is."

"Am I to join everyone in the factory?"

He sighed. "You've heard more than you should, but your papa's gone and gotten himself into...a delicate situation. It's just 'til we can afford to send you to the Academe."

I frowned.

Something about this town didn't feel temporary--the way people's drooping shoulders matched their mouths, the way buildings held a hint of desperation with their creaks and wobbles. This town didn't release folks to bigger and better things. It kept them tight within its clutches.

Forever.

A shiver pricked goose pimples along my arms, and something deep within the earth made my nose itch.

"What is it?" Papa asked, and I shook my head.

There was no reason to be suspicious of someone using magic, but after Mr. Ashton's reaction to the word, I tucked away the reminder to investigate further. Something just wasn't right in this town.

MY DISAPPOINTMENT WITH THE LACK OF BELLS WARRED with curiosity the next morning. The factory doors towered far above my red head. Moss grew between the doorframe bricks, and rust stained the mortar. When I stepped through the doorway and didn't feel magic's touch at my feet, I sighed. A shove from behind sent me sprawling face-first along the floor's dead planks.

"You're blocking the door. Get a move on." The gruff voice's owner shuffled past me, leaving me a spectacular view of worn boot-heels and a coarse gray cloak. My mother's frizzy hair blocked my view of the factory as she knelt, her hand thrust out to take mine. If my mother had been a magic user, the owner of the worn boots would have needed a new pair. Instead, she helped me to my feet and glared as others passed.

From the disabled who hobbled in with canes clutched in knobbed fingers, to the mother with a baby strapped to her hip, women and children of all ages and sizes filed into the factory.

Large looms stretched nigh the full length of the floor, crammed against each other. Wedged in each corner rose four staircases. Women settled into their weaving with a simple rhythm while the children lined up against the front wall.

"You must be the new ones," said a man with a scruffy beard tucked into the collar of his shirt. My gaze landed on the top of his balding head, and I hid my grin. "You--" He jabbed his finger at me. "Join the other children."

My mother inclined her head, and I trudged over to stand behind a girl shaking rain out of her cloak. The man with the long beard led my mother toward the building's rear, and I shivered in the damp chill. "Who was that?" I asked the girl before me.

"That's the Tackler."

"The what?"

She tilted her head toward the looms. "Looms are in-intra-inter--"

"Intricate?"

"Intricate machines. When they aren't behaving, the Tackler fixes them to work so them on the looms can weave. You're the new one, aren't you?"

A girl older than my fourteen years shushed us as the Tackler approached.

"Good--you've already met Charlene," he said.

The blonde folded her cloak and set it on the floor without response.

I pulled mine tighter about my shoulders. "Yes, sir--" His thin nostrils flared, and I ceased speaking and joined the others in a rigid line that snaked around the interior walls.

We followed him silently--not that it would have mattered much with the looms' racket. The queue stopped beside a woman who pumped a foot treadle as her deft hands spun wool through the loom's grid. The Tackler gestured to a girl at the front of the line. "You turned sixteen yesterday, correct?" The girl who had silenced me earlier nodded. "You'll be working with Rebecca to learn the loom until you've developed the skill to weave on your own."

The girl's cheeks flushed at what obviously was intended to be praise, and I bit my tongue. Nothing about this job piqued my interest. A hundred or so women sat on hard stools in silence as they worked with hand and foot in a loud, drafty room. My mind itched for my books, but I followed along wordlessly as the line resumed its movement toward the rear of the building. The Tackler opened two doors and ushered us into a room the size of our old home in Devlon.

I followed Charlene to two stools against the wall. "I'm Elise."

She nodded and pulled two stiff-bristled brushes from a nearby basket. Charlene handed them to me and asked, "Ever carded wool before?"

"Never in my life."

She raised a brow and shoved a small basket of wool into my lap. Her demonstration with the carders proved thorough, but when I tried my hand at it, the wool caught in the spines of the brush. "You're pulling too hard. Be gentle," she said. She stretched the wool until it formed a uniform swath moving in a single direction. Thirty strokes later, mine remained a mass of fibers moving at odds with each other.

"It takes practice?" I asked. While Charlene shrugged, several children hid laughs behind oily hands.

"My ma says your ma used to sew for fancy ladies in Devlon. Is that true?" asked Charlene, and I nodded. "Then how'd you end up so...unskilled?"

I smiled. "My gran says I was destined for greater things."

It had been a point of contention between my mother and my paternal grandmother--right up until she had passed the year before. My gran had studied magic until she had married at her parents' insistence. It was her wrinkled fingers that had first touched mine to the soil and taught me of power.

The gentle lull of brushing the wool relaxed my shoulders, and my head dipped toward my chest until Charlene kicked my ankle. I jerked my head upright to find a woman old enough to be my grandmother in the doorway. I squirmed beneath her gaze until a few giggles caught her attention. "Remove your cloak," she barked.

"I'll catch a chill. Please, I'm not used to...such conditions."

More giggles, which she silenced with a look. Despite her bony frame, strong fingers tugged at my cloak and forced me to my feet. Both carders clattered against the wood floor. I towered over her and with the hunch in her back, she struggled to look me in the face. I straightened my cloak.

The others stared at their wool with rapt fascination. "You're new, so I'll forgive your insolence today. But tomorrow, I expect better. You aren't well-to-do no more, so don't be expecting no favors. Tomorrow, you'll leave your cloak with the rest."

When the doors closed, Charlene released the breath she'd been holding. "Is that woman normally so cross?" I asked, but she rotated her stool until her back was to me.

To keep myself awake, I sketched incantations in my head and wordlessly recited formulas until my hands were stiff and my stomach threatened to pierce my backbone with hunger. When two o'clock arrived, the other children pulled lunches from their satchels. Their meal was punctuated by brief whispers. My feet were nearly numb after half a day on a wooden stool, and I bent over to touch my hands to the floor before rolling up to a standing position. My hand was on the chilly doorknob when someone touched my shoulder.

"Where're you going?"

A boy stood behind me, a roll of bread between his fingers. "To find my mother," I said.

"Can't." His hand against the door kept it firmly shut.

"But my mother has my meal."

"She'll be working now. Her lunch brief was at one," he said.

"I promise I won't bother her. I just wish to fetch my lunch from her bag."

An old puffy scar beneath his eye twitched. "You'll have to eat later. Can't interrupt the weavers."

"But--"

He pried my fingers from the doorknob and once free, pressed one of them against the puffy scar beneath his right eye. "If you interrupt the work, we all suffer, see?"

I jerked my finger away and returned to my stool, though my stomach grumbled audibly. Charlene handed me a wedge of cheese and some dried apple bits.

"Thank you," I said.

"No, thank you."

I got the feeling she was thanking me for remaining in the room, and I asked, "Is it like this every day?"

"Like what?" she whispered.

"Silent. Dejected."

The boy with the scar pressed his lips together, but otherwise ignored us. "There's too much to do for idle chat," she mumbled as she nibbled on a hunk of bread.

"I've never worked before, but surely you could talk while carding-- at least as good as you are."

Someone shuffled by the closed doors. Once the person passed, Charlene asked, "You've never worked?"

"No."

"Then whatcha do before?"

"I went to school."

Scar boy laughed. "We've all been to school. What did you do after that?"

"I'm not referring to the elementary standard. I was studying for entrance into the Academe." When Charlene cocked her head, I added, "The Arcane Academe of Veleden."

Two dozen children edged their stools away from me. Those still seated on the ground drew their feet under themselves. "Don't tell anyone," said Charlene. "Magic isn't allowed here."

"Why?"

The boy with the scar strode over and stopped an inch from my face. Mutton and the hint of apple soured my nose. "If you want to survive, stop drawing attention to yourself. Stop asking questions."

"But questions are how one learns--"

"Not in Dekwood."

This time, when the shuffle returned to the door, it didn't pass. The old woman stepped inside, a brown satchel in her hands. "Your mother made quite the fuss 'bout you gettin' this." She thrust the patchwork bag in my direction.

No one in the room glanced at the old woman, but they were aware of her every movement. Even the seven-year-old in the corner watched from the corner of her eye. I took my meal, but I was no longer hungry. How could I survive this town? How could my parents?

Charlene would accept none of my lunch, not that there was any time. We returned to our labors after little more than three bites. The older children shifted from carding to spinning the wool into long threads on spindles. By the time work ended, my arms and back ached. No one complained, nor did they limp or tremble as I did.

My mother's pale head bobbed in the mass outside the room but quickly disappeared as bodies shuffled toward the drafty building's exit. My shoulders brushed against silent townies, and I'd nearly reached the front door when something tugged on my cloak. I had neared the doorframe when I felt another tug.

"Elise," someone whispered, and rough hands propelled me through the door. The bright sun made my eyes water until Charlene's gray form blocked the setting sun. "Elise, I needed to warn you to be careful."

"What reason would I need to be cautious?"

Charlene bit the edge of her lip. "Stop asking questions."

Before I could pry further, she vanished into the throng of workers. Someone tapped me upon the shoulder--my mother. Her shoulders drooped like decayed flesh. "I used to enjoy weaving." She rubbed her expanding middle and frowned. "I hope your father doesn't mind another round of the restaurant's corned beef."

Dinner bearing the consistency of an eraser didn't rest easy with my mind or my stomach, but my muscles screamed for sustenance and rest. It would have to suffice.

Like toy soldiers we formed a line that marched from the factory into the center of town, and from there, bodies separated to their homes without chatter or smiles. As my mother and I trudged toward the inn that served as our temporary home, snowflakes began to fall.

PAPA MIGHT HAVE POSSESSED THE PATIENCE FOR CORNED beef, but little else that evening had given him pleasure. My questions about the oddness of such a town had fallen by the wayside, as had my complaints about working in the factory rather than preparing for the Academe. His words were placations for ears too young to comprehend their warning.

My ability to attend the bells that evening had waned as exhaustion had set in. My eyes had closed the moment I had tucked myself beneath the scratchy woolen blanket.

When sleep released me the next morning, the inn retained its usual silence and my parents' room lay empty. On the table rested a scribbled note bearing Papa's scrawl.

*If you felt like I did yesterday, I figured you deserved the day off. Use it for study, eh? Your mother will tell the factory you've caught a chill. I'll be at work if you need something. There is some bread and cheese in the breadbox.*

THE CHEESE WAS A TOUCH TOO SHARP AND THE BREAD JUST this side of stale, but they numbed my hunger. Outside, snow coated the cobblestone road and dotted the rooftops white against the gray sky. Tempted as I was to stroll past the factory and stick my tongue out at its closed door, the opportunity for a "holiday" pushed sense into my head. Besides, the crudeness of such a gesture would have set my mother to vapors.

The streets were as devoid of children and merchants as the day we had arrived. The town held its breath as its people worked--though for what purpose, I couldn't see. I tucked myself between two buildings and pressed my hand to the cobble, but the crumbling stone blocked any tingle of magic.

The door to the factory protested as it opened and closed, and I tried to sink into the cobble behind me. Charlene frowned at me from the alleyway's end, and I relaxed.

She said, "I thought you were sick."

"I caught a chill but upon waking, felt the air calling to me. Perhaps it might lend health to my lungs."

"Is that magic talk?" she asked, and I inclined my head. "See, that's the very thing that won't sit well with the magistrate."

"What would I care if the magistrate takes pleasure in my speech?"

She leaned against the building and closed her eyes. For all her youth, her frustration aged her and the eyes she turned on me could have been my mother's. "Take care, Elise. People who don't know their place tend to disappear."

"Disappear how?"

"I shouldn't say, but...it's only fair that you know, being new. Have you heard the bells?"

I shivered. "I tried to listen for them our first evening here, but they never came."

Charlene's eyes widened. "Be glad they never came, Elise. Be glad! What do you know of them?"

"Nothing much. Everyone in Dekwood fears them, which makes little sense. Christmas approaches. We should be ringing the bells to welcome the coming of a new year and the gifts of our health and fortunes. To remember the dead and celebrate the future." Her eyes darted to the road as if she expected something, and I tilted my head. "Charlene, why do you dally with me? Shouldn't you be at the factory?"

"I was sent by the Tackler to search for you."

"For what purpose?"

She glanced a third time at the snow-covered street. "To make sure you were being truthful when it was said you'd taken ill." My snickering carried, and Charlene reached up to clap a hand over my mouth. "Shhh, they'll hear you."

"Who? The factory workers? Drafty though the walls may be, they would hear naught over the looms' thrum."

"No, not the workers. The Ringers."

"Beatrice, the innkeeper, spoke of something unnatural in the bells. I've heard talk of spells that can commune with our ancestors but never with foul intentions. Are these Ringers spirits then?"

"They aren't living. I don't know what they are."

The alleyway dimmed, and I flattened myself against the wall with Charlene. Our movements hid little as the innkeeper glared at us. "I knew you were up to no good. And Charlene--" She jabbed a finger at the girl, whose bottom lip trembled. "--what would your father say to hear you've been talkin' about things better left unsaid? Do you wish to court trouble this close to Christmas?"

The girl squeezed past the innkeeper. I placed a gloved hand on my hip--a gesture my mother would have abhorred--and nodded in the direction Charlene had darted. "I do not see what business it is of yours what Charlene and I discuss."

"Charlene should be at work in the factory, as should you." The innkeeper stopped my sideways motion with a firm grip on my elbow. "Your family's new here, so you don't understand our town and our ways. But the Ringers aren't nothin' to laugh at, and if you know what's good for you, you'll leave it well enough alone."

She didn't stop me as I brushed by, but my insides quaked. I expected a child to fear the boogieman looming in the shadows, but for an adult to fear one so, lent credence to the idea that it was more than a mere spirit or specter--possibly something magical in origin.

Possibly something more dangerous than I was prepared for.

I could have returned to the factory like the young woman my mother wished I was, but I could not. Magical study drew rule breakers and thinkers--people who wished to make order of magic's chaotic nature. If I were to understand these Ringers, I needed information.

And for that, I was going to need my books.

MY LIBRARY RESTED SOUNDLY INSIDE THE WORN LEATHER chest in my room. The dull buckle remained latched, though the chest had been pushed away from the door. A basin held fresh water from the innkeeper's visit to my room, which was perhaps when she had discovered my escape.

Papa's employ had provided us a certain level of influence in our previous home of Devlon, though not as much as my mother had wished. Despite our more affluent standing, we were held in little regard by those with true wealth. We had ignored my mother's ostentatious nature while saving up for my first year texts at the Academe. My fingers remained gloved as I removed both books from the chest.

The *Livre de Cantus* held the basic foundation for magical studies, and I set it aside. *The Histoires de Créabet Magia*, though, bore the history of magics and creatures of the known world.

I was convinced the answer lay within its pages, but several hours passed, leaving me with nothing more than a stiff neck and aching shoulders. A two-sentence paragraph on the probable existence of ghosts was the only reference to the undead in the entire tome. Nothing on bells or creatures with bells that caused people to disappear.

Information on the undead required a library-- specifically, a library with the books of the grand arcanum. A town this small wouldn't have one...or would it? The first day we had arrived, I had felt the thrum of magic.

Downstairs, the innkeeper's fingers were lost to a pile of yarn and knitting needles. She ignored me until I stood beside her, then she glanced up from her needles with a cocked brow. "Do you need somethin'?" she asked, needles still clicking.

"Does this town have a library?"

The yarn wrapped around her index finger stilled. "Do you need a book to keep you company during your...illness?" I nodded, and she fetched a hardbound book from beneath the bar. "This here's a new mystery. Just finished it last week."

"I was hoping to choose my own reading material--" Her scowl deepened, and I retrieved the book from her waiting hand. "Thank you. But if I finish this and wish to read more, is there a library in town?"

"Not enough folks in town read for a library to be necessary. Ol' Henry does us right enough."

"Ol' Henry?" I asked.

"Local trader. Comes by once a month with whatever he picks up out in the world. A few books, some fabrics and yarns, random bits and things. You make sure that book takes no harm. Cost me a scarf and a good bottle of wine."

If someone possessed the books I needed, they weren't sharing. But then, most of the town kept tight lipped. The needles resumed their clicking as I left the inn. Only one person had opened up to me, and she was at the factory.

THE FACTORY'S FRONT DOOR LOOMED LIKE THE COMING snow, and as I crept through, I waited for the Tackler to pounce. His shiny head never made an appearance, though one elder worker nearby thwacked her knuckles on a loom's wooden frame as she worked. No one glanced up, but they shivered in the cold wind that accompanied me through the entryway. The looms' humming drowned out the closing door's snap and those of my footsteps as I sought the rear carding room.

One left turn too many had me lost.

In front of me stood a woman whose wrinkles carried wrinkles. Rather than throwing a wooden shuttle through the floor to ceiling loom, the woman used a metal rod to weave bright colored wool by hand. She hunched over her weaving, her nose nearly touching the wool, and added tiny starburst patterns to a bright blue sky.

"I'm sorry to interrupt, but..." If she heard me, she made no indication, and I stepped closer to the loom. "I said I'm sorry--"

The old woman set the rod aside and cocked her head. I tried again. "I'm Elise, and I appear to be lost." Her mouth moved with slow, exaggerated movements but without sound. "I don't understand--"

"You'll get nothing out of her," said a rough voice. The boy with the scar stood behind me, a basket full of washed wool in his hands. "So many years in the factory, everyone goes deaf."

"She tried to say something. Or at least I thought she did," I said and followed when he gestured for me to do so.

"She was just mee-mawing at you. You'll need to work here a span longer than a day to understand all that nonsense. Besides, I thought you were sick."

My cheeks grew warm despite the chill of the building. "The illness passed, so I decided to return to work."

His basket full of wool bounced, and he pursed already-too-thin lips together. His expression read, *you'd-have-to-be-insane-to-come-back*, but I shrugged it off.

"I became lost and decided to ask directions. What is mee-mawing?"

"The loomers talk without sound, through lip-reading and miming, though I suspect sometimes they just make it up." We turned right where I had turned left and ten feet later, we stood before the double doors to the carding room.

Charlene dropped her carder when I entered, and one of the older girls behind her said, "I thought you said she's sick."

I ignored the jibe and took my place beside Charlene. While yesterday had proven a quiet affair, the youngest children chattered in the corner while those older and nearing apprenticeship gossiped in whispers. I leaned closer to Charlene. "Is it true there is no library in Dekwood?"

"I think there's one in Magistrate Leunt's mansion. My dad mentioned it once. Why?"

"My books lacked the details on a particular research, but if I could perhaps look it up, that may give me answers. How do you function without a library or proper schooling?"

Charlene glanced up from her wool, but no one paid any attention to us in the hum of conversation. "Magistrate Leunt says there's no need for school beyond the basics. What use would we have for such knowledge working here?"

"But haven't you ever wondered why the sky is blue? Or why the snow only falls in the winter?"

Charlene shrugged, but her eyes lit up like buds on spring trees.

I asked, "Or why the trees outside this town have died?"

Several voices paused, awaiting Charlene's answer. "I..." She glared at the boy with the scar--who shared the same pointed chin and green eyes. Only a sibling could level such a look that flushed her skin, but Charlene was daring and she answered me in a quaverless voice. "I asked my dad once why other towns live with joy and food and warmth while ours shrivels like the forest outside. He wouldn't answer."

Air whistled between clenched teeth, and the boy with the scar crossed the room with a dozen steps. He leaned over and whispered something in Charlene's ear.

"No, Matthew, I won't be quiet," said Charlene. "Elise's right. Why don't we have a school anymore? Why is magic forbidden if it's a gift from the gods?"

She rattled off a litany of questions, but my brain latched onto one in particular. *Magic forbidden? It really was forbidden here?* I'd never encountered such a rule or law, but the idea made sense when added to people's reactions. Lost in thought, I missed the door opening and the hush that draped across the room. Something rough slapped my motionless hand, and I tumbled back into the real world.

"--Asleep again? Why aren't you working?" The woman before me lacked an arm, yet her single hand was rough, her fingers bearing the same calluses of the other weavers.

She raised her hand to slap mine again, and I shook my head. "My apologies," I muttered as I dragged the carder across the wool in my other hand. The woman nodded, but her narrowed eyes followed me as she paced. For ten minutes the room held its breath and worked, and only when the disfigured woman departed did the group return to a hesitant chatter.

Charlene's breath tickled my ear as she leaned close. "My father has a few books. I...I might be able to get them for you."

"Thanks, but I'm looking for something in particular."

"I know, that's what I mean. I've seen them--they have special covers and--"

I clapped my hands over hers to still them. "Wait, your father owns books on magic? Why would your father have those?"

"You met him the other day at the statue. He works for Magistrate Leunt."

Matthew cast aside his work and returned to Charlene's side. He hauled her up by bony wrists and dragged her into the corner where the youngest children worked. "You'll sit here until you can learn your place," he said and glared at me as he fetched her carders.

My fingers tingled in the cold room. The wooden floor kept me from the earth's soil, but moisture licked the air and brushed my cheek with the echo of magic. Air was trickier--thinner and more temperamental--but I set aside the carders and splayed my fingers across the surface of the air.

At first, my fingers remained chilled as I whispered the word for warmth, but after a few minutes, my fingertips flashed with sudden warmth. Sweat broke out across my forehead and trickled down my chin.

The air rose a degree at most before the energy fizzled. I slumped over, my breath haggard. Children stared and whispered. Across the room, Charlene's mouth hung open.

"Get back to work," snapped Matthew.

He did not look in my direction, but the edges of his shoulders and chin left me trembling. Rather than thanks for a warmer room, the children left me in frigid silence. At day's end, Matthew whisked his sister away before I could inquire further about the books. My mother frowned to see me but must have noted the tension in my shoulders as we left. The walk home remained as silent as my afternoon had been.

I pled out of another corned beef dinner, instead choosing to curl up with the book the innkeeper had loaned me. My eyelids drooped as I turned the pages of yet another boring text that lacked the magic and adventure of the real world. The light peal of jingling bells reached my ears as the book fell against my nose, but when I opened my eyes, the sound was gone. Morning had come.

I'D GROWN ACCUSTOMED TO THE HUM OF THE LOOMS AND the hiss of their whispers. When they vanished, my ears grew acutely aware of the bitter silence in the factory. Before, villagers had offered brief smiles and nods to each other on their way through the front door. Today, no one made motion to do more than shuffle in and stand. Waiting.

But waiting for what?

My mother squeezed my collarbone too tightly, and I squirmed until I tumbled free to skid to a halt before the Tackler. Whereas he normally tucked his lengthy beard beneath his shirt, it rested atop it this morning. His collar was buttoned too tight against slight jowls as he cleared his throat. "Today serves as a warning to us all," he said as he flicked his gaze in my direction. "Everyone plays a role in Dekwood, and when someone doesn't know their place or steps out of it, they're a danger to our way of life. A danger to us all."

A dozen workers over, a woman stifled her sob. The Tackler sought out the source and finding nothing, continued. "Don't let loose the grieving thoughts that plague you, but instead, put your mind toward the task at hand. Christmas approaches."

The voices that recited his words lacked enthusiasm. "Christmas approaches."

The phrase transformed their faces. Where there had rested sorrow and fear, grim determination lit a fire in their eyes as they departed for their workspaces. My mother shrugged as the masses carried her away from me.

"No trouble today," the Tackler barked at me, and I frowned.

I remained silent until I spotted the empty stool in the carding room. "Where's Charlene?"

Matthew's lip welled with blood where he'd bitten it too hard. I repeated the question, this time while staring directly at him, and the carding brush in his hand snapped in half. "Let it go," he muttered.

"Where is she? And why did the Tackler profess such warnings?"

Like yesterday, they were destined to ignore me. I scooted my stool beside a little one stuffing hunks of wool into a basket. "I don't think we've met. My name is Elise. What's yours?"

"Belinda."

"Don't speak, Belinda. The bells will come." At Matthew's sharp warning, the child wrapped her arms about her legs, her eyes wide.

In the back of my mind, the bells jingled as the moon rose, and I dropped my carding brush. "Matthew, the bells did come. Last night--did they not? Tell me, where is your sister?"

He closed his eyes. "The bells shook the air last night, and the Ringers walked among us. I thought they'd come for you--" he said, stopping to look on me with tearful eyes, "--but they'd come for C-Charlene."

This was my fault. I'd encouraged Charlene to talk against her better judgment, and because of it, she was gone. "I-I'm sorry, I did not mean--"

"Didn't mean what? To talk Charlene into her death? Because of your talk of schools and magics--as if such things were possible in Dekwood--she went home and begged to be sent away. Can you imagine? She asked *our* father to be sent away so she could learn!"

Anger flushed my cheeks. "Matthew, I never intended for your sister to be taken, but asking to learn should not be a crime. Where exactly has she been taken? By whom? What are Ringers?"

"The Ringers ensure the peace and prosperity in this town. They make sure everyone serves their purpose. When they...they--when they take you, you're dead, Elise. Gone."

I did not recall when I stood, much less when I fled that room, but my running ceased when I reached the smallest building near the center of town: a lone house befitting someone who served Magistrate Revoir de Leunt. Its bricks crumbled a little less, were a little less faded than those around it, and instead of a single-floor dwelling, the house was its own two-story abode. The wailing from inside--a harsh, keening of pain that carried on with few gaps for breath--confirmed my suspicions.

The front step creaked beneath my foot when a shadow moved behind the window, and the same slip of a man from our second day in town leaned out the open doorway to wave an empty fist at me. "Go away! Haven't you done enough to this town?"

"I'm sorry?"

When he laughed, the wailing inside grew louder. "You watch it, girl. They'll be coming for you next!"

His words should have scared me, but the fluttering inside my stomach ceased as the earth beneath me hummed. Somewhere out there, someone called on the magics deep within the soil. Someone out there was not as backward thinking as the villagers. Someone out there was educated.

But not Nicolas. For all Charlene's belief that her father owned magical texts, not a single drop of power sang in his blood or whispered in his breath.

To him, I said, "I am quite sure they will seek me out, sir, and when they do, I have questions for them."

"You won't be able to ask."

"Why?" I asked, and the crying inside paused.

"Because when they come, they suck out your soul." He retreated and slammed the door behind him, but not even solid oak could drown out the cries inside.

Death magic. It had to be.

If the Ringers took ownership of people's souls, then for what purpose? Fuel? Something to power the dark magics required for the undead to walk the earth? Who would do such a thing? Who could?

I stared at the shadowed mansion that hovered in the distance. The only person people feared outside the Ringers was the magistrate. He possessed power and money enough to control an entire town. And if the rumors were true, he was ancient and learned--learned enough to make my knowledge of magic a mere thimbleful.

The thought filled me with dread.

No matter what words were uttered, Papa stood firm. "Their ways aren't ours, but we're here now. Keep your head down until we send you to the Academe. "

"But Charlene is missing." My mother's chair scraped across the floor as she excused herself, and I asked, "What reason do we have to remain in this town?"

"Just a smidgen longer, Elise."

"Papa--"

He closed his eyes a moment. "We owe the magistrate for putting us up here. To leave would be a mark against us."

"Do we need his favor so much then?"

Papa sighed. "A man like that--he'd keep you from school with only a frown. Don't court trouble. By mid-spring, summer at the latest, we should have the means to leave."

I fled, crossing the hall to my room. He had never been a man of excuses before, any more than my mother had allowed her appearance to falter or her tongue to still. Sleep avoided me as I stared open eyed at the cracks in the ceiling until long after the hum of my parents' conversation changed to snores. When snowflakes tapped against my room's tiny window, I rubbed the sleeve of my nightshirt against the pane to stare out across the town below.

The street should have been bare this late hour, but diminutive twinkles danced in the air, cast off from the shimmer below. Rather than look away, I gaped as five white horses took form beneath my window. Five muzzles snuffed the falling snowflakes. One shook his head and sent up an eerie peal as the bells on his harness jingled--less a jingle and more like the scream of cold air across one's skin.

These weren't mere horses, and the five men astride them weren't mere men.

Red coats clung to gray flesh that stretched too taut over skeletal frames, and the mouth that grinned at me tugged at the corners until it might have split the near-translucent skin. This Ringer--his blue eyes ghostly and glowing--bore a sash across his red jacket, decorated with symbols burned black into the fabric.

Even from the inn's second floor, far from the touch of the earth, the thrum of magic in the air seeped into my feet. The bells rattled my ears as the horses stepped forward.

I flung my heavy jacket over my nightshirt and stuffed my socked feet into my boots. I threw open the door. Halfway down the stairs, I recalled the hour and slowed my steps to a creep.

The bolt was thrown over the inn's entrance; I shoved it upright with a grunt.

By the time the bitter chill outside blustered my face and threatened to rip the air from my lungs, the Ringers were gone.

Snow filled in the edges of the hoof prints. I followed them down the main street and around the corner toward the edge of town. In the distance, the forest darkened an already dark night, and I closed my eyes before I stepped across the town's threshold.

If they'd crossed into the forest, I'd never find them. Something...or someone...whined to my left, and I followed the sound into a partially fenced yard. Tucked back against the trees lay a house made of lean-to boards and half-rotted wooden planks. A sagging roof groaned under the snow's weight and out front stood five white horses. I hurried my steps.

Inside the house, another whine, then a cry, and the air outside warmed. The snow stopped, and my feet sweated inside my leather boots. Magic. *Dangerous* magic.

I didn't know what kind, but the power of it made my vision swim. I stepped sideways to avoid the horse droppings. Horse droppings? Where they real beasts then? One of the horses shoved his muzzle into my shoulder blade, and I flinched.

The horses were living creatures. But what about the Ringers themselves?

My hand paused on the curtain that served as the house's front door. When a child screamed, I stumbled over my boots as I pushed my way through thick wool. Five beings who had once been men shimmered in the main room. One stood over a child no older than four, who cowered in his mother's arms. Tears stained the child's reddened cheeks and snot gummed up his nose, but no sound or breath escaped his blue lips.

His mother screamed at the Ringer, and when he touched his knotted hand to her flesh, her lips parted round.

I snapped my eyes shut, and inside my boots the soles of my feet burned.

Outside the air split with a cacophony of jingling bells, and when I pried open my eyes, two corpses lay in the corner, their hands tangled in one another's.

They weren't vanished or disappeared as Charlene had implied.

They were dead.

※

"WHAT DID YOU DO?" PAPA'S VOICE CARRIED MORE THAN A warning with the question, and I winced.

"There was magic; I could feel it! I needed to see what these Ringers were about," I said. My mother tore apart the roll in her hands, leaving little breadcrumbs scattered across the table's edge. Preoccupied with watching her, I failed to see Papa move until his hands seized mine in too tight a grip as he stood beside my chair.

"Don't follow them again. Leave it alone. Promise me now."

"But--"

"Do as you're told!" he snapped, and I tugged my hands away. "I'm-I'm sorry I snapped, Elise, but this is dangerous. This isn't growing a tree in the backyard or blossoming a flower in a vase. It's dangerous magic-- the kind that comes with decades of learning and leads to evil beings and death. A-and I can't lose you." His voice caught, and what was left of my mother's bread fell to her plate with a thud.

"I need more time to clear our debt to the magistrate. Please mind me," he begged, and I nodded. After that, neither of my parents ate.

When my mother and I walked to the factory that morning, we passed the coroner's carriage. A trio of men moved two bodies wrapped in blankets--one child-sized and both bundled with care.

"Is that...?" my mother asked.

"Yes."

She wrapped an arm across my shoulder and squeezed. "Listen to your father, Elise. Please."

Up ahead, Papa spoke to Mr. Ashton. Whatever words Mr. Ashton spoke caused Papa's face to pale.

"We'll be late, Elise."

"I'll catch up," I said to my mother, who placed a hand over her swelling middle as she clambered through the snow without me. Papa furrowed his brows when he spotted me, but I hid in the shadow of the coroner's carriage until Mr. Ashton retreated.

"Why aren't you with your mother?" Papa asked when I finally approached.

"I forgot something. Was that Charlene's father?"

Papa nodded. "We're moving out of the inn in a few days' time. Probably after Christmas. Magistrate Leunt has found us a place."

My stomach sank. "Where?"

"Just at the edge of town. It's in rough shape, little more than a lean-to at the moment, but they're going to repair it for us. Can't have your mother expecting in a place as drafty as that. Now hurry along to work."

If the cold air hadn't made my teeth chatter, the news would have done so. The home that would be ours had belonged to the two victims, and the thought of dwelling in such a place sickened me. Would our taking such a home further indebt us to this magistrate?

Papa watched me until I had turned the corner, but I waited twenty heartbeats--long enough for him to leave-- before I returned to the statue at the town's center. There was something about this mysterious magistrate we never glimpsed--this magistrate in charge of a town of fear and death.

Animating the dead wasn't impossible, but it was forbidden for a reason.

I glanced into the statue's face. *Are you behind this?*

The stone eyes blinked.

I tumbled backward to land on my rear in the snow.

"It's how he knows." The voice belonged to a man buried in rags reeking of body odor. He ran a hand through graying, oily hair that hung a few inches past the tips of his ears.

"Who? The magistrate?"

"Who else? The man in control. He watches. He listens. And when you ain't right, the red men come."

"The red men? You mean the Rin--"

The hand he clamped over my mouth soured my stomach; it stank of blood and earth. I wriggled, and he pulled his hands away. "Don' say their name. Gives them power."

"What are they? Are they reanimated corpses or something more?"

He shrugged. "Does it matter? Until Christmas passes, no one is safe."

"I know things, sir. Magics. Basic practice, but I could--"

The man shrank back at the word. The coroner's carriage stopped beside us, and a gentleman in a crisp, black suit approached. "Mr. Henry, come with me. It's time to see to Elizabeth and the boy."

The man's face crumpled at the name, and he allowed himself to be ushered into the carriage and away from the watching eyes of the statue.

The carriage set off in the direction of the mansion. If there were answers to be had, they would be there.

No magician worth his salt worked without a library. No one. It was long past the hour to discover what this magistrate was hiding, though it would have to wait. Another day's work missed would be noticed.

The hours dragged along as I carded wool in silence. Everyone gave me wide berth, and for once I did not mind. Papa spent dinner alternating between peering at me from behind his soup spoon and pausing with his mouth open, though he said nothing at all.

That evening, when I watched behind the frosted glass of my window, the Ringers and their horses materialized directly below me. The shortest one, with green eyes of a color that could melt hearts, peered at me beneath his red cap. When he hooked a finger and beckoned to me, I threw the shutters closed with a snap and fell beneath my covers until the jingling bells faded, and the sun crept over the horizon.

Christmas Eve had begun.

I abandoned the inn before the town awoke and sought the lone path to the mansion. While I thought myself alone, red weaved itself against the drift covered trees and cobble. In the light of my oil lantern, I thought the trees painted with blood until the red moved. A person perhaps?

The figure ahead turned his green eyes on me.

He was alone, Ringer though he was, and when he beckoned for me to follow, my boots crunched in the fresh snow as we approached the mansion.

A grand porch of white stone led to wooden doors bearing stained glass depictions of angelic figures. Circular turrets framed the house on either side, topped by clay-tile spires and iron finials. When the Ringer's boot heel touched the first of twelve steps, the stone didn't shift, nor did the snow depress under his weight.

"Wait!" I whispered, but he gestured at the darkened porch. "I know, you want me to follow, but...are you real?"

His deep green irises marked his sorrow, and he inclined his head once. I reached out a trembling hand to touch his coat's fabric, but he leaned away from my grasp. His breath came in little puffs as he pointed again to the front door.

He did not progress beyond the first step, though his muscles strained and tugged as if he wished nothing more than to proceed. A small eight-pointed star was burned into the left side of the door frame, and when I touched it, it burned my thumb through my gloves.

"You can't pass...because whatever ties you to this world is here? In this mansion?"

His direct look intensified the burn that coursed through my thumb. "S-s " He grimaced as his tongue hung from the side of his mouth. "S-s-sa-save."

"Save? Or safe?"

"S-save us. All." The bells called out in the distance, and he clenched his hands at his side. "Save."

His figure wavered before it disappeared, and the snow fell in earnest. The doorknob turned beneath my hand, and the door swung open to an entryway of shadows and silence.

Was I expected? Or had the Ringer opened the door?

I muffled a cough in my sleeve as my dry mouth choked on the dust floating through the air. The steps of a grand staircase were draped in rugs long since faded and crushed. When nothing beyond the dust moved, I released my breath in little puffs that danced before me in the chill.

Melting snow left droplets along the wooden floor as I approached the first door on my right. A seating area, followed by a dining room with a table long enough to fit our family, cousins included. Beyond that lay the kitchens and pantry, a smaller eating area, a second living area, and a music room. My fingers lingered on the grand piano, leaving dust trails across the black and yellowed keys.

My breathing quickened, and the wind creaked through invisible gaps in the walls as I approached the grand staircase. The old rugs muffled most of my footfalls as I ascended to the second floor, and once there, I paused outside a room whose open door left a sliver of light in the hallway.

I nudged the door an inch, and when no one shouted or leapt at me, I opened it to a room clear of dust and loneliness.

The library.

Shelf-lined walls held books with gilded covers and lettering in more languages than I had ever seen. In the center of the room, a single desk rested, its velvet-lined top devoid of stationery or ink. The first bookshelf held histories of one kind or another, and I had almost skipped it when I spotted the eight-pointed star near the top: a heavy volume whose cracked spine read *The Accountes & Affairs of the Famile Revoir du Leunt.*

Once I had coaxed the book from its shelf, I settled into the corner with an unobstructed view of the doorway. Not that there was anywhere to hide, but it might have been possible to tuck myself underneath the desk. I squinted at the cramped handwriting on the first dozen pages. Mostly accounts of births and property acquisition, I skimmed first paragraphs until I spotted the pattern of dots in the top right corner of each page.

16: 05, 06, 07...the counting of years or months? The code was familiar to me from my studies. The halfway point of the book held the date of 1693, so supposing the dots' arrangement meant years I flipped to the last page, which was blank.

Was the magistrate adding to this book? I backtracked until I reached pages bearing a style of loose-flowing handwriting that was lengthy in stroke. The last entry was dated almost a century ago in the year of 1743. Blotch marks sprinkled their way across the yellowed page, and the handwriting shifted as his emotions overwhelmed him:

*My boys--all dead--Nothing good and pure and wholesome comes from a woman, this one more than most as her wyld and evyl ways brought my young Eli to ruin. There is naught more foolish than a young boy in love, and doubly so when in love with a sorceress.*

*She thrice scoffed him before the town and his brothers rose to his aid, as brothers should. For nigh two hours they battled this sorceress and sought to drive off her evyl spells from this village, but ne'er had they fought with such a foul creature.*

*I came upon their bare bodies in the centre of town, my sons' corpses drained of life and warped by magics far darker than taught by decent sorcerers. And she stood above them, her smile as grim as the winter's new sun. I will remember her words until my death.*

*"Your sons thought to best me, Magistrate Revoir du Leunt. I merely wished to walk alone, but Eli would have none of it. Obsessed he was. An unhealthy and unholy sickness was upon him."*

*Sorceress she may be, but my family's history she knew not, and I smote her where she stood. The ground reached up and buried her in its gaping jaws, but still my sons were dead. Still their bodies lay tossed like stones across the river top.*

*Tonight, they will wander the land of the dead no more. Tonight, the earth will return to me what was lost, and this town will harbor sorceresses no longer.*

THE WRITING CEASED, THE FOLLOWING PAGES BLANK. NOT that it mattered. An event over a century ago involving our magistrate--

the same magistrate, if the names were to be believed, had cast his sons into the realm of living dead. The skill required to create such beings...

I slid the book back into place. Three more bookcases held a variety of stories and treatises but nothing continuing the family story. Certainly nothing magical. On the last bookcase, I spied a collection of magical texts. Rather than focus on their concealed titles, I shut my eyes and whispered my fingers across their spines. Power ebbed and flowed from them, but my fingertips did not tingle until my hand rested on a slim book wedged between a behemoth of a text and the edge of the shelf.

There was more than power to this book. There was hatred and envy and sorrow.

A well-worn yet simple cover--nothing to call attention in a grand library such as this--yet when its pages fell open at my touch, spells of death and life were sketched in grand detail. I shoved the book into my pocket, though it was not far enough away from my heart for comfort.

My lantern flickered as its oil burned low, and I crept away and down the stairs. As I tiptoed with aching, cold feet, I spotted a lengthy picture on the wall whose frame hovered an inch or two above the carpeted floor. An ugly beast all claws and teeth gnashed his way toward the edge of the canvas. In the opposite corner, a woman cloaked in red velvet crouched, her hands glowing as she fought the beast. I removed one hand from a glove and touched the painting.

Nothing. No response.

But it had to be here! Wherever his workroom lay, it would be on the ground floor. Somewhere that would touch the soil of the earth and open to the air and water of the sky. I set my lantern on the floor and, gripping the painting by its frame, tilted it. Behind the painting, the wall was missing.

The weight of the painting near tipped me on my side, yet I heaved it from the wall above to expose the open archway. As I leaned it against the wall, I prayed no one would awaken to notice the painting's misplacement. I brought my lantern into a narrow stairwell that smelled heavily of iron. A dozen steps down brought me to a metal door, which was unlocked.

The bottom corner dragged across the floor with a cry, and I winced as I wrenched it open. Nothing moved above or below, and I stepped across the threshold into an almost empty room: four bare walls, one archway walled off, and one wobbly-looking chair in the corner. The lone window near the ceiling confirmed I was in a basement. The perfect sorcerer's workroom.

Yet no sigils decorated the sparse room--not even the eight-pointed star that had burned my thumb.

A shift in weight caused the stairs outside to groan. Someone stood outside. I dragged the chair to the window. Even on my tiptoes, I struggled to push the window up and open as its jambs stuck. Outside, bells jingled and a set of hooves stopped before the window.

The Ringer with the green eyes touched the glass, which dissolved with a gust of snow and wind. I pulled my upper half through the window frame and received a face full of snow. More of the powder wiggled its way into my coat as I shimmied through. My jacket caught on the latch, and I gave it a firm tug before tumbling outside.

Something old and angry mumbled inside the room I'd vacated, and the ground beneath me trembled. With no care for the tracks left behind, I tossed up snow as I bolted toward town. Halfway to the inn, the bells ceased, and the earth shook no more.

My breath struggled in my chest until I crawled into my bed, and even then, my thumb throbbed with warmth.

⚜

I SLUMBERED LONG PAST THE RISING SUN AND WOKE TO shoulder shakes. When I opened my eyes, the shaking relented, though my mother sat on the mattress's edge as worry lines traversed her forehead. "What time is it?" I asked.

"Long past when young ladies should still be lying about. It's near noon."

Her words brought me upright in bed, and I cast aside my blankets in a rush. I crawled over the footboard and around my mother. "Why aren't you at work?" I asked as I dug through the bedside chest.

"I was. I came to check on you. You aren't ill again, are you?" She pressed a cool hand against my forehead, which I shrugged aside in order to pull on a pair of stiff pants. My mother scowled but said nothing about my choice of attire. Tufts of wool clung to her shawl, which she pulled closer about slumped shoulders. I glanced one-too-many times at my bed, and my mother crouched with a groan. Her round belly brushed against the mattress as she tucked her hand between it and the wooden frame. She would have liked to have been up to her shoulder in her search, but my soon-to-be brother didn't allow for it. Either way, she rooted around quite unladylike and undignified.

The woman who'd always taken such care with her appearance resembled the rest of the town--shoddy, rumpled, and tired. Her pointed shoes were faded and scuffed, wisps of pale-blonde hair had escaped her bun, and the bottom of her gray skirt was torn. Whatever nonsense the magistrate used to hold this town in disarray had to be stopped.

My mother's hand came back empty, but I held my breath rather than allow the sigh to escape. She reached for my arm to pull herself upright. I frowned, and she waved her hand in the air. "I thought--never mind. I need to get back to the factory."

Her heavy steps lumbered down each stair step and once she had arrived at the bottom, I retrieved the book I'd "borrowed" from the very back corner of the mattress. Simple bound, black leather with only the title etched in silver lettering: *Mort de Vie*.

Cold as it would be outside, I could not be caught reading this. My boots went on first, followed by my heavy wool coat, then a cream-colored scarf that reeked of mothballs, and matching woolen gloves. Lastly, I tucked the small book into my coat pocket and set out for somewhere quiet.

Despite the pallor over Dekwood, the sun glinted off the snow, nearly blinding me as I headed for the edge of town. No one would think to seek me out at the house that eventually would be ours, especially not with repairs set to begin after Christmas.

The heavy curtain was missing from the doorframe, making me glad for my coat's warmth. I avoided the living area where the mother and child had been killed. The sun trickling through a wedge of window cast shadows where they'd lain, and I hurried my steps into the next room. The stove held no warmth, but I drew my own as I noticed a child's letters scribbled across scattered paper on the table. My smile faltered when I studied the page.

The little boy had sketched images of the Ringers.

I leaned on the chair, and when it didn't break, I took my seat and retrieved the book. Its innards lacked the printed text of most books on magic. This one held an older, shakier handwriting. Assuming *The Accountes & Affairs of the Famile Revoir du Leunt* had been penned by the magistrate and his predecessors, this work was by someone--or *something*--else entirely.

Most of the pages held spells--not just incantations or minor cantrips to light a candle or put a hound to sleep--but spells with real power: the kind I'd never see in school, the kind I wouldn't discover until long after I'd grown gray and crooked after the magic had corrupted me.

One spell cast the soul of another into that of a beast, while another claimed to keep all ills at bay. When I turned the page, I dropped the book on the table where its spine splintered. *Clochen Mort de Noël.*

Death bells.

It was more than the cold that chilled me as I read. The half I comprehended was enough.

> Upon the evenfall of Solstice, submit five upon the land.
> In the holy circle of Elshirei, draw forth the
> innocent and pierce the air with peals of five:

> Thy will it be,
> five blind will see.
> A year unmade,
> until the spade,
> doth break this circle
> of Christmas that's made,
> And set the risen free.

THE CIRCLE WAS EASY. EVERY SPELL TIED INTO THE EARTH, into the land, but to create a circle of blood to honor Elshirei the Betrayed was an unclean deed. To raise the dead--

A hand touched my shoulder, and I screamed.

"Please, I didn't mean to frighten you." Mr. Henry hovered beside me. The rags he wore stank of booze, but he turned alert eyes on me in that moment. "I knew I felt something--"

He pressed a finger to my thumb, and the burning pulsed. "You've been to the house," he said.

I nodded. "How--"

Mr. Henry rolled down the collar of his scarf to display the *viziol* branded into the bluish skin on his neck. The protruding V, which rose from the top of two nested triangles left me slack with relief, and he shook his head. "I know that look. You think I'm here to save you, save this town, but I'm not."

"But you are a sorcerer, trained in the arts of high magic and served with protecting..."

Tears welled up as he cast a glance over his shoulder. "I've done my duty to this world and look where it got me. Elizabeth and Peter dead-- their souls used to keep that filth alive for another year. When tomorrow passes, I'll be one more among the many and gladly so."

"Please," I said as he turned to pass, "Tell me what this is. I don't understand this spell or how to stop it."

He laughed a rich, belly laugh. "If I can't stop it, what makes you think a mere whip of a girl like you can? You've not even earned entrance to an Academe, much less gained an apprenticeship."

"I-I...may not be able to cease this spell's grip, but I must try, Mr. Henry. Please tell me what this spell means." I pointed at the paragraph in the book and the drawing beside it of the reanimated corpse with dull eyes and bells tied at its belt loops.

"I can't work the magic anymore, not for a long while. Something the magistrate's doing, I suppose."

"Were you sent here to stop him?"

He shook his head. "Not me, but my grandpa. He gave his life failing, as did my pa. That madman stripped the magic out of folks after that, but there's something...something deep down. A rumbling perhaps. I can feel it in the earth." His breath smelled of rot, and I took short breaths through my mouth. "He's losing control of his boys."

Outside, the wind gusted, and the planks rattled around us. Mr. Henry didn't notice the goosebumps that decorated his bare arms.

"His boys?" I asked.

"Them horsemen--the bell ringers. Those are his sons he's brought back."

"The story then, it is true? About the sorceress killing his sons?"

Mr. Henry nodded. "Rumors are that his sons deserved it. Either way, that spell's how he did it. At first, the mighty Magistrate Leunt did the killing. He slaughtered four women in their sleep that morning--all of them sorceresses--and used the blood to draw his circle. Did it at the Solstice's dawn, the day after his boys died. He anointed silver bells--it must be pure silver mind you--with the same blood and spoke the words. It near killed him from what I've heard, but then, he'd already had spells in place to protect against that."

"How...how old is he? The magistrate?"

"Older than this town. Or maybe not old enough. It doesn't matter." I closed the book, and Mr. Henry nodded. "Good, get your folks out of this town and away from this madness."

I slipped the book in my coat pocket. "I am not leaving. I am going to break the spell." His laughter drove icy air into my resolve, but I stood straight. "A Ringer asked me to try, so I must."

"Now I know you're nothing but silly. The Ringers can't speak."

"But he did--the one with the green eyes--he asked me to save them."

Mr. Henry tilted his head. "Huh. Maybe the magistrate is ready after all. Too many centuries passed him by in his sorrow. Look, if you're determined to do this, it must be tomorrow."

"On Christmas?"

"On the Christmas."

"Why?" I asked.

"The Ringers feed to replenish the circle's seal between Solstice, when they rise, and Christmas, when they sleep. Look again at the spell."

I retrieved the book and turned to the proper page. Mr. Henry pointed to tiny scribblings near the edge of the page. "The blood cord protect for five full days," I read, then shook my head. "I don't understand."

"To renew the seal, he must remove his protections."

"...And the circle will be vulnerable!"

He nodded. "But you still have to get to it. He'll see you coming. He has his eye on you yet, I'd wager."

"I'm counting on it."

"MOTHER?"

She laid aside her knitting and waited. How she found the energy after a long day working the factory loom was beyond my comprehension, but every evening since we had arrived, she prepared for my brother's birth. "Hmmm?"

"I need you and Papa to do me a favor." Papa, who'd been stretched out across the bed, sat up, eyes open, and I swallowed hard. "In the morning, I need you to gather the folks in town at the statue. Get everyone to bring all the bells they can--silver bells--"

"Is this about those funny fellas in the red coats? Didn't I tell you to stay away from that evilness?"

My toes curled in my stockings at Papa's questions. "How'd you know about their red coats?"

"Saw them just last night."

"If you see them again, flee. They are killers."

"That's what Frederick at work said. I know I told you to keep your head down, but something wasn't right with how they looked. I couldn't get warm after seeing them." He stared at his knees.

"They are the magistrate's sons, Papa. They died over a hundred years ago, but he brought them back from beyond. He uses the town to keep them alive." The entire story poured forth and by the time I'd finished, my mother was tossing her belongings into a chest. "What are you doing?" I asked.

"Packing. We're not staying here," she muttered.

"That's not a bad idea. Papa, you two should leave. At least until Christmas passes."

"And what makes you think you aren't coming with us? Debt be damned," he said.

I left their room and crossed into mine where I retrieved the book from its hiding place. When I returned, I closed their door behind me and set it on the table.

"What is that?" Papa asked.

"It is a book on dark magics. Foul spells that call for the murder of innocent people. I found it in the magistrate's house."

My mother hissed, "You trespassed?"

"I had to know what purpose he served in--"

"And now that you do, you'll what? Use that book against him? If he's really as old as you say, you won't touch him with the little tricks you know. Besides, no daughter of mine will commit such...ungodly acts!" Papa had found his feet halfway through the tumble of words, and the door slammed as he left.

My mother's knitting needles remained untouched on the table beside the book. "What will you do...if I gather the townspeople?"

"The Ringers will seek out the statue--imagine, a town full of unwillful people-- and when I hear the bells, I will know he is vulnerable. I will break the circle with a single smudge. The spell will be broken."

"Surely it can't be that easy."

"Magic is organic. It comes from the earth and the air, the beings around us, and our will. If you remove any of those components, magic dissipates and returns to its natural state. The circle can't be protected if he means to renew it."

I withheld the mention that I'd be trespassing...again, not to mention the danger of crossing a magical circle, vulnerable or not.

She shook her head, and a gray curl fell across her cheekbone. "I'm not sure I understand it, but if you say you can do this, I believe you. Everyone will be at the statue on Christmas if I have to drag them there at needlepoint."

I snatched the book from the table and turned away so she wouldn't see the tears in my eyes.

THE CRISP MORNING OF CHRISTMAS DAWNED ACROSS Dekwood-- the one day of the year no one worked. Families would gather to eat and celebrate the coming of a new year, of new opportunities, and new beginnings. Sometime after sunrise, Papa would wake as usual and give thanks to *Wothan* for the sacrifices made in our honor. The town, assuming they followed tradition, would sacrifice five cattle--cows if they had it, though sheep would also honor the All-Father. While children dreamed of the gift giving to come, I crept from my bed and into the pre-dawn's falling snow.

Five horses stood in the field nearby, their bells removed as they pawed through the snow for whatever grasses lay underneath. The magistrate's mansion felt hollow to the touch, but where else would a mourning father be but here with his sons?

He would expect me through the front door--that plan would fail. I backed down the steps until my boots touched soil, then I slid first one foot and then the other from my boots. My stockings came next until I shivered barefooted in the snow.

While my feet froze, my skin hummed with the power beneath me. Around the mansion's side, the basement's window waited as paneless as I had left it. The room stood empty, but the chair had been returned to the corner. I drew a circle in the snow with an ungloved finger and picked up a pinch, which melted in my hands. The water droplets returned to the snow as I whispered.

Inside the room, the chair wobbled.

Sweat broke out across my brow, and I removed my wool hat, which I stuffed into my coat pocket. Nothing could leave the circle, not even to join the pile my boots and stockings made nearby. I dug my fingernails into my palms and focused.

*Move the chair. Move the chair.*

Still the chair merely wobbled.

The barest hints of sun peeked over the horizon, and I closed my eyes to the distraction. The chair trembled. A light scratching as it then slid an inch and another. I panted as drips of sweat sprinkled to land inside my circle. A thud of wood against stone rang out, and I opened my eyes.

Without breaking the circle, I leaned forward and peered down. The chair rested against the wall a few inches to the left of the window. The power drained from me in a rush, and I broke the circle with my chilled finger.

Despite the ache in my toes, my boots remained outside as I slid feet first through the window. I landed too hard on the chair, which fell over and toppled me on my side. Inside the empty room, I sighed and rubbed my hip where I had landed.

Nothing led to the location of his circle. The floor was cold stone, smooth and polished and completely unyielding to my probe for a power source.

I took out the silver ring in my pocket. It had been a gift from my parents, the single piece of silver to serve as the root. If I wished to study at the Academe, this ring was required to cast the compulsory entry spell. An expensive cost for our family but worth the price.

If I used it now, I might never set foot in the Academe.

Two bodies haunted me, and I whispered. The power inside the ring hummed and warmed my fingers. I allowed the warmth to wash over me, and when I brushed my fingers along the wall, a bell on the other side cried out in pain.

"Open," I whispered, and the silver ring dissolved into vapor. The air around me sizzled, and the stone wall wavered five heartbeats before disappearing to reveal a workroom. The walls remained of gray-slab stone, but the floor was compacted dirt and lacked the typical smells of manure and greenery. I poked a single finger in it and listened.

The soil was dead.

A rut formed the circle, its insides rimmed with fresh blood. At its center lay a single bell. Simple and plain, with no ornamentation and a single dent. The bell's original bloody baptism had long faded. I couldn't cross the circle, not yet. Not if I wished to remain living.

Again a squeak on the steps alerted me to a guest, and I leaned against the wall and breathed while my muscles screamed to flee. My feet burned as someone halted outside the visible doorway.

"It's been far too long since there's been a touch on the soil other than my own."

The voice was rich and deep and reminded me of my late grandfather. Far too kind a voice for someone exercising such atrocities.

The man who stepped inside lacked the wrinkles his retreating hairline professed he should have. When he glanced at me, his eyes lacked his voice's humor. They carried the empty framing of winter, cold and dead.

I stepped away from him, careful not to touch the circle. The magistrate followed me, and I edged as close to the circle as I could. When he touched the top of my head, my vision swam. "So like her you are," he whispered. "And like her, you've stolen away Eli."

"Eli?"

"My son. He should ride the town with his brothers, yet he hovers behind to watch you. He always carried a heart sickness within him. Horsewhipped by the mere sight of a woman."

I melted under the layers of clothing: rugged pants tucked into men's boots; a plain, button-up shirt; and a coat hanging past my knees. No curves, nothing pink, and certainly nothing womanly about me. "I'm more likely to be mistaken for a boy than a woman. I've not distracted your son, sir. He wishes to die."

"He's already dead."

"Not completely. The bell ties him to this world. He wishes to rest."

The magistrate stepped across the circle. "Simpering fool was always the weak one. Maybe it's time to replace him." He reached for the bell.

"Wait!" I shouted, and his gnarled hand stopped mid-reach. "Why do you keep them animated like this? To serve what purpose?"

"To serve life! My sons were unfairly and untimely ripped from me at the prime of their youth. Why ask such questions though, when you already know this having been in my library."

His thumb smudged a blood droplet as he retrieved the bell. It sounded once, and Eli materialized before us. I scooted closer to the door until my back leaned against a workbench. Now that he was within the circle, I could not break it.

Eli's green eyes glowed in the room's dimness. "Kill me," he whispered, and the magistrate clenched his fist around the bell.

"After all I've done for you and your brothers, you truly beg for death?"

I glanced over my shoulder. A lantern flickered on the table.

While Magistrate Leunt argued with his son, I reached back and grasped the lantern by its base. Its heat burned my fingers for a moment before I tossed it across the circle's threshold. Its glass casing shattered, and the spilled oil caught in a bright flash of flame.

"Dammit," the magistrate muttered and shoved the bell into his pant pocket. He removed his jacket and used it to beat the flames. Eli swiveled and nodded once in my direction. My thoughts were correct.

Arrogant as the day, the magistrate had failed to protect against non-human physical intrusions.

While he danced with the flames, I smeared my bare foot across the dirt and broke the physical circle. The shock drove the magistrate to his knees as the circle howled, and I retrieved the bell from his pocket.

I had but a minute before he would recover, so I made the only choice available to someone as thoroughly outclassed as I was--I ran.

Boots abandoned, I pounded up the stairs in quite the unladylike fashion. The bell in my hands rang louder than my footfalls, and I burst through the front door as I struggled to listen over the sounds of my haggard breath. Halfway to the statue, I heard them.

Bells.

Hundreds of bells rattling and clanging and jingling as the sun blessed the Christmas day. Behind me, hoof beats on the road approached.

Mr. Henry had clambered up to the statue's arms, where he beckoned for me to hurry.

Between gasps, I shouted at him, "The horse's bells...are ringing! Why...Why haven't they...stopped?"

"We need a circle!" called Mr. Henry.

My feet were nearly numb, but the snow's sting sharpened my focus. There was no time to draw a circle this large. "Quick, make a circle! Shoulder to shoulder, and ring the bells!" I shouted.

Some villagers stopped ringing their bells when they spotted me; none of them made an effort to form a circle beyond my parents, and even they cocked their heads at the request.

The Ringers stopped before the group, and several villagers dropped their bells. A child cried--a whimpering hiccup that awoke the town to the danger before them. Several stepped back while others made motion to leave.

Mr. Henry stopped their flight by clapping his hands together. "Here's your chance. You can fall prey to the Ringers, or you can do what she says. Make a circle and keep ringing those bells! For Elizabeth and Peter and Charlene and countless others we've lost to the bells."

Like a well-manned loom, they circled around the statue with each person's shoulder pressed up against the next as they rang the bells of Christmas. I stood in the middle and called out to Mr. Henry. "Now what?"

"Destroy the bell."

"What? How? The power--"

"Is broken. It's just a bell."

One Ringer reached for the woman in front of him. I held the bell in both hands and snapped its wooden handle. Both pieces tumbled to the ground. Blood coursed off the silver to pool in the snow. The Ringers shrieked--ungodly sounds of torture and joy--yet one set of green eyes found mine. Tears pooled in Eli's eyes as he smiled.

A few villagers paused in their ringing, and Mr. Henry cried out, "Keep ringing those bells."

I fished the bell out from the bloody pool and wiped off the remaining droplets with the corner of my jacket. Once clean, I held the bell by its crown and gave it five chimes.

Five brothers faded from the world. Five sets of bells fell tarnished to the snow below.

And in the distance, a disheveled man rode toward us. I pushed my way through the villagers until I stood as a shield before them.

They filed in behind me, a united wall as the magistrate approached. His years weighed on him like sand; his skin sagged as he dismounted. Each step grayed his hair until it flashed white, and his shoulders curled in on his frame until he hunched over--one lone man before the people of Dekwood.

"Magistrate?" a woman whispered, and he cupped a hand to his ear. "Say again?"

"Do you know where you are, Magistrate?"

He frowned at her. "No, where am I?" His eyes blinked. When he met my gaze, recognition lit them. He raised a finger in my direction, but Mr. Henry placed himself before me. The *viziol* on his neck pulsed.

"Your magic has returned?" I asked.

He nodded, and the magistrate flinched. Mr. Henry touched his thumb to the old man's forehead. Five counts before the magistrate cackled and tumbled away. His feet carried him to his horse. The effort would cost him, but he mounted swiftly with another cackle. His horse's bells released a sour note as he galloped for the forest of the dead.

"Should we pursue him?" I asked, and Mr. Henry shrugged.

"The spells he used have warped him. Hard to say whether he has any real magic left."

"Good riddance," someone cried, and others muttered similar statements.

My mother draped an arm around my shoulder and pressed her lips to my head. I shivered in the Christmas sun. "Can somebody fetch me some shoes? I seem to have left mine behind."

Laughter draped the village in a glow, and behind me, someone said, "Dearie, you can have whatever you want."

Spring brought life to the village. My mother gave birth to my brother, Saul, and the village of Dekwood established Mr. Henry as the town sorcerer. They bestowed the magistrate's mansion on him, though he never set foot inside. Rather than linger with the illness such dark magics cast upon a place, he rebuilt his home at the edge of town and set about restoring the success of its people.

The magistrate never returned to Dekwood.

Some believed he could be heard cackling madly in the forest of the dead, which never grew again, while others said he blew away in the wind that swept over the village in the coming days. Others still told tales of his voice ringing out in the highest pitches of the jingling bells deep in winter.

The bells returned no one, but their jingle held a bitter sweetness for the people of Dekwood until such a time as they forgot the Ringers. When the villagers kept their fear no longer, the forest returned and the looms sang songs of the people's bravery. They smiled to think of the magic that had saved them.

And the red-headed girl behind the magic.

About *The Ringers*

Originally published in *Joy to the Worlds: Mysterious Speculative Fiction for the Holidays* (Grey Sun Press) and later reprinted as a standalone novella, *The Ringers* came from another conversation with my partner. (This happens a lot!) We were discussing how prevalent bells are in holiday music, and they asked me what if the bells were harbingers of something malevolent. That night, my brain spit out some images of The Ringers and off I went with a new story. Something about the idea spoke to me of fantasy Victorian villages and Dickens style writing. I love gothic literature so consider this my love letter to it.

# COOKIE MAN

Coffee shops can be an interesting smorgasbord of characters, especially when you're a writer. You see people, and the mind takes off, creating backstories and plot lines to go along with the coffee that was spilled and the tea to go at 9 AM. Any given day, there's the redheaded woman, who conducts business meetings completely in Russian from her normal spot at the back table; the soccer mom with twins, who is more interested in her phone than the kids spilling water all over the front counter; the flamboyant gay man who wears pink proudly and loves to talk about sports; and then there's Cookie Man.

Based on his slouch, slow movements, and wrinkle-content, I imagine he's at least an octogenarian, though I suppose he could be seventy-eight just as easily. Several times a week, he trudges into Uptown Coffee to meet his daughter. Or his much younger girlfriend, I'm not quite sure which. Neither order coffee. Not ever. He orders a water and a chocolate chip cookie, warm please. She gets the Earl Grey tea, though she might as well be ordering the water as that particular brand is no Twinings.

I don't know her name any more than I know his, but for the purpose of this tale, I'm going to dub her Whipper, as she reminds me of a character by that name from an old 90's show. I suppose this woman could be Dyan Cannon, the actress who plays the character. She's got the blonde curly hair and overly thin build that wrinkles instead of building muscles or fat like everyone else as they age. Somehow I doubt it. No one else seems to notice her the way they would a celebrity.

Three times a week like clockwork, these two come in and order, sit together, and chat for an hour. Then they go their separate ways.

One unusual morning two weeks ago, Whipper arrived to Uptown before Cookie Man. While waiting for her tea, I stand nearby awaiting mine as I chat with the barista. Whipper's curious about what I called "gruesome" and is surprised to learn I'm discussing a book instead of the newest "horror movie." She inquires after the plot, how far along I am in its writing, and the typical questions a writer gets asked by strangers.

This eighty-pound woman sporting a smart business suit once dreamed of being a writer. "I wanted to write children's books once," she says. "But life got in the way. I never went back to it."

Before I can inquire further, Cookie Man arrives. He's not one to appreciate waiting, so her attention shifts to him. His smile is genuine, but when there's a line at the counter, he frowns like a five-year-old fit for a tantrum. I suspect he more closely resembles a toddler these days, but Whipper handles him well.

I find it cute the way she dotes on him, and damn if I still can't tell if she's the daughter or girlfriend. They sit in wooden chairs, their conversation quiet and private for such a public place, and once the clocked turned over, they were on their way: he to the left and she to the right of McGraw Street.

Last week was a buck to my system. For two months straight, every weekday found my ass planted in a corner of Uptown Coffee. I can't help it.

Does it help the writing? Sure. But more than that, I'm curious. These two have a story, and I'm determined to learn it. But when my partner becomes sick, I stay home to take care of her for a few days. Tuesday brings my return to Uptown, but only me. No Cookie Man. I guess he isn't a Tuesday sort of guy.

I spend the next day dealing with the mundane: car mechanic appointments, grocery store trip, and all the rest of the boring tasks we do through our lives. By the time I reach Uptown, it is long after noon. I manage not only to miss Cookie Man and Whipper, but all the morning regulars.

I think nothing of this as I'm there to work and work I will. Unbeknownst to me, my perceived disappearance has created quite the stir. Both Cookie Man and Whipper have continued to quiz my poor barista. "Did she finish her book? Is she not coming here anymore because she's done?"

"Is she ill? When did you see her last?"

She held no answers for them, so they exit as I turn the corner. Almost stepping on Cookie Man's bare feet *(yes, he walks barefoot)*, I stop with an apology.

Cookie Man stares at me through coke-bottle lenses, his overly large eyes a pretty blue. "Are you The Writer?"

Not "A" writer, but "The Writer," capital-T, capital W.

I nod, a bit taken aback that he knows who or what I am *(though on retrospect, I suppose she told him about me)*.

He seems so involved in the process of heating his warm cookie, picking it apart for the chips first and then the rest, and I hadn't been aware he'd even noticed me, let alone anyone else in the coffee shop. Aside from Whipper that is.

"We were worried about you! Hadn't seen you in a while," Whipper said, patting Cookie Man's shoulder like one would to comfort a child.

"Did you finish your book?" he asked. "That great big 500-page one?"

"Not yet. I probably will today, and it's up to 560 pages now." I couldn't help but grin at how his already huge eyes widened further, the whites slim circles around the blue.

"Good! Tell me what it's about."

His excitement contagious; I couldn't help but oblige. The plot line poured out of me like Seattle rain. Despite his age, he stands patiently, absorbing every word until I finish. Then he smiles, his dentures reminding me of my own grandparents. Grandparents who listened to anything and everything and loved every single word from your mouth until they were gone.

A precious commodity.

The gaze Whipper gives him parallels my own, joyous and slightly amused with his childlike glee.

Cookie Man pats my shoulder with wrinkled, crooked fingers as he nods. "Good," he repeats. "Keep writing! Do you have a publisher yet? When can we read it?"

"I don't have one yet. I—I still need to revise it and such, but hopefully soon," I say, holding up crossed fingers.

He tries to cross his own but his arthritis prevents it. Instead, he points down to his bare feet where his toes are crossed. Mostly anyway. My own laughter echoes across the intersection. The overwhelming need to buy this man a cookie washes over me, but before I can offer, he speaks again, still grinning like a fool.

"Keep writing, even when you're done with this one. Keep being a great writer." And then they move on, Whipper holding his arm like a movie star on the red carpet, head held high as she walks alongside his shuffle. She leads him across the street and on to wherever their next adventure lay.

I suppose one day I'll return here, and the Cookie Man will be no more. Like my own grandparents, gone. Dead and buried. No longer reachable to hear the words of children and dreams. But for now, his bare feet walk this Earth, and I am overjoyed in this knowledge. This character, as so many who pass in and out of these doors, can only encourage and inspire. My personal cheerleaders. Whipper and the Cookie Man.

She's definitely the daughter.

If I still had a grandfather or father like that in the world, I, too, would feel famous. Like a million bucks.

They cross 33$^{rd}$ Ave, and when he turns left and she walks to the right, their parting brings tears to my eyes for a moment.

I want to shout, "Hold onto him!" But I don't speak. Instead, I return to the counter, ordering my coffee with a return to normalcy and the rest of the characters of Uptown.

*Time to write.*

ABOUT "COOKIE MAN"

This story is an exploration of blog meets story. There really was a Cookie Man, though he sadly passed in 2016. "Whipper" is still about and no, she's not his daughter. Just a good friend. He does have a son living in Seattle. Something about their story tickled me. It was too cute not to write about in some way, so I decided to experiment with the structure of it.

# AMASKAN

Fifteen years old and still the memory of her parents' murders stung. Homeless and starving, her elder brother had discovered his young sister sleeping in a dirty alleyway. Long since a member of the Order, he'd convinced her to join him with a chunk of fresh bread and cheese.

Fifteen minutes was how long it had taken her to pick the lock the first time she'd tried it. Provided she could pull herself together enough to survive the trials, she would join him in the Order of Amaska. Her fingers shook, and she almost dropped the thin rod to the cobble below.

Fifteen hours ago, she'd been little more than a trainee but now... Now everything mattered with a sharpness that left her gasping as she stood in the dark alley, the night's air her only companion.

*I must pass the test, if not for my sake, then for my brother's.*

The rod shook as it slid into the lock. Her skin crawled as a few leaves fell to the ground, and she forced herself to ignore her body's reaction. The only shadow that watched her was her own.

Polished iron, the lock was a simple thing—nothing difficult really —the sort of lock one would find on half-a-dozen middle class homes across Sadai, yet her fingers continued their nervous habit.

The wind stopped and in the silence, a slight gasp sounded from the other side of the door. She paused until the sounds passed before resuming her work. Narrow notches across the rod's top knocked against the lock's interior, and the spring compressed beneath the rod until a subtle click announced the lock's submission. She turned the knob half-an-inch before the breathing returned.

*If he breathes any harder, he'll be hyperventilatin' before I can get this damned door open. Leave it to my mark to be an insomniac.*

Shendra counted to ten. Twice. She was halfway through a third count when the footfalls shuffled away, and she cracked the door open enough to access the hinges, which she smeared with grease. Likelihood of squeaks averted, she slid through the open door.

Darkness shrouded the front room, but light drifted in from a narrow hallway ahead. Any floorboard could betray her, so one slippered foot before the other, she prowled her way across the room as she listened. When the shuffling from the hallway picked up, she pressed her back against the wall and held her breath. The mark passed by the open doorway. A second door opened and closed behind him, and after another dozen heartbeats, she peeked around the corner.

*Nothin'.*

No servants. No furniture. Just a long, narrow hallway with two doors at either end.

At least it would be easy. The mark had no escape other than through her. Shendra's muscles quivered as she passed through the corridor with all the speed of a Boahim Senate decision. She scowled at the thought of the senators—*cowards, the whole lot of 'em.* For all their talk of justice, they'd done little more than frown at her parents' murders five years ago.

The door stood before her, and like tomorrow's mission, it filled her with trepidation.

*Dammit. Get it together.*

Another pause, another reason to doubt her ability as an Amaskan. *A real Amaskan would've been in and outta here in a few heartbeats. Some killer I am.*

She pressed her face against the wood grain and listened. Small hiccups pierced his light breathing as he drifted in and out of a shallow sleep. The rod wasn't needed for the interior door, as the knob turned gently beneath her hands. More grease was applied to the hinges, but the next heartbeat proved it wholly unnecessary. One foot into the bedroom, a hand gripped her upper arm tight enough to bruise.

"You're dead, Shendra. You've failed."

The candlelight reflected off Bredych's blue-gray eyes, and Shendra leaned her head against the door's hard oak, her black hair falling forward to cover her face. "I can't fail tomorrow. I don't know what's wrong, but I couldn't stop shakin'."

Her brother tilted his head at the trainee playing "mark" in the bed, and the young man fled. Once the front door shut, her brother frowned. "Somethin's off for sure. All that shaking, I could hear the rod in the front door. You havin'—" He bit off a curse before correcting himself. "Are you having second thoughts?"

She rolled her eyes. "I don't know why you bother fixin' it. Not like anyone cares if you talk all proper when you're killin' 'em."

"They might. If you're sent into a job that requires it. Besides, you avoided my question."

The sigh that escaped only reminded her of the tension between her shoulder blades, tension that ran straight down to the balls of her feet. "I-It's not that I'm havin' second thoughts so much as havin' third and fourth thoughts. I mean, I'm gonna kill—"

He pressed a finger against her lips, his grin a cold flame. "There can be no doubts, sister. None. Fail enough and they'll—"

"Kill me. I know."

A snap announced the front door closing, and they both flinched. "Guess Master Elish is here," said Shendra, and a moment later, the bald man stepped into the hallway, broad chest leading the way.

Master Elish stared down his bull-like nose at his trainee. "Considering the tension in your frame, I suspect something went amiss with your practice run?"

Like her brother, Bredych, Master Elish's frown aged him, a reminder that they both carried more practice in the art of killing someone. She leaned back into the room's shadows, shoulders slouching. *And Bredych wonders why I have doubts about committin' myself to the Order. It doesn't matter what I tell myself, this still feels like murder.*

When Bredych's elbow connected with her side, she recalled her master's question. "Bredych caught me enterin' the bedroom, Master."

"But first I heard her pick the lock. She still hasn't mastered it."

"I'm feelin' out of sorts tonight, Master Elish. Been thinkin' a lot on my folks." The lie flew easily from her lips. Yes, they'd been on her mind, but her stomach chased circles around her doubts—the real reason for her distraction.

"Families are a liability, as they have proven to be tonight." The rebuke was deserved, so she said nothing as they followed Master Elish from the training house. Her black wraps clung to her tall frame in the heavy air outside. Shendra tugged at her silk-wrapped wrists as they trudged up the hill towards the Order's main building.

She might've been dressed like her brother and Master, but everything else was a harsh reminder of her future here. Their bald heads and jaw tattoos marked them members of the Order, but it was more than that. The way they moved—almost flowing across the ground—and the way they carried themselves with a confidence that spoke of commitment to their calling. Shendra sighed.

Despite the late hour, most training areas glowed with torchlight as fellow trainees drilled in the arts of assassination. For all that Master Elish refused to use the term, it fit. The Order of Amaska might've served Justice, but killing someone—no matter the reason—was still murder, not to mention a crime against the Thirteen. The knots in Shendra's stomach twisted tighter, and she touched two fingers to her forehead. *Thirteen lead me to thy will.*

"Relax," Bredych whispered as he kept pace with her fast steps. "You're too obvious."

It was easy for him. At thirty-eight, the Order was more than a way to make money. They were his family and his passion. Besides, he'd never minded doing what was necessary to get along in life. Shendra slowed her steps.

Two Amaskans stood guard at the main building's entrance, and they nodded to the group as they passed. The casual seating area lacked its usual occupants, and Master Elish gestured for them to join him in the entryway's empty chairs. "Your preoccupation with family created a failure today. Will you be ready for tomorrow?"

"Yes, Master." Another lie, this one less easy than the first.

"When is she not ready?" Bredych said as he twirled a small twig between lanky fingers. "This is my sister we're talking about."

Tonight was the wrong evening for the joke as Elish turned sharp eyes on them both. "We have much to discuss before the trials tomorrow."

A small group of trainees approached carrying an undignified amount of giggles with them as they passed. Her brother waved, missing the tension in Elish's shoulders. Her master's exact age was a mystery, but the Order's records estimated near sixty—an easy to forget fact when training with him left her one long, walking bruise the next morning.

But this evening, the way his right leg settled awkwardly across his left knee reminded her that more than her own future within the Order was at risk. If she failed, his bid to be the next Grand Master would be ground into dust. After all, if he failed to train her successfully, how could he lead the Order? Shendra exhaled, allowing the air to sweep away the weight of her thoughts.

"For nearly five years you've sheltered and trained with us," Elish said as he followed her gaze. "And for that long, you've never been as quiet as you are this evening. If you truly wish to commit yourself to the Order, I ask you to speak your thoughts plainly, Shendra Abner."

The laughter in her brother's eyes fled, and his feet ceased knocking against the chair leg as he stared at the wall over her head. "I—" She paused as Bredych's thoughts leapt up and danced unspoken before her. He might as well have been screaming. "I'm not sure the Order is the place..."

The charred remains of her sentence withered to the ground as her Master frowned at the old debate. "So your brother was correct then. Your family still weighs upon you. I would remind you that it's far too late for this, Shendra. Either you will be reborn into the Order tomorrow, or..."

Maybe she could find a moment to leave before morning arrived. One glance at her Master made her doubt the idea, and she nodded her acceptance.

"I told you she was ready for tomorrow," said Bredych as he grinned.

Normally his smile was contagious, but this evening his lips were the only ones turned upward.

Tomorrow, she'd become an Amaskan or she'd die trying.

DIM LAMPS MADE FOR DARKENED HALLWAYS AT THIS HOUR. Shendra paced the hallway outside the small meeting room. "I can't believe ya told him," she said to Bredych.

"What else could I do? Something was obviously chewing on you, and if I didn't speak up, it would have been my ass on the fire right along with yours. Or had you forgotten that part?"

"I've not forgotten, but what makes ya think you've any chance to be Grand Master? Yer not even on the council yet! At least Master Elish has a chance at the position. At least *he* has a reason to be worried 'bout tomorrow."

The parchment's weight in her pocket felt heavier than it should, and her finger ran along its edge until a sharp sting answered. The pain settled the turning in her stomach.

Bredych sighed. "I wish you woulda said somethin' to me. 'Bout your doubts."

His reversion back to their childhood tongue reminded her of their mother, and the pain in her stomach returned. "When Ma died—"

"Don't."

"When she died, I had nothin'. Ya were the one who convinced me I'd find a home with the Order, but I only did it to be with ya. Yer all that I've left in this world. Without you, I'd've ended up at Lady Essia's, and we both know it."

"So why doubt the Order if we gave you a home?"

Shendra pressed her forehead against the cool, stone wall, and her dark curls hid her tears. Tomorrow, if she passed the test, her hair would disappear along with her freedom. "It's not that I regret gainin' a home and a family, but at what cost? I'll never be Shendra again. Everything that's me will disappear, and in its place will be an Amaskan. A killer. It's one thing to speak of killin' and another to actually do it." She was aware of his hand moments before it rested on her shoulder and resisted the urge to shrug it off. "I'm not talkin' about the horse manure I repeat to the Masters 'bout servin' Justice. I'm talkin' about murder, Bredych. A woman's gonna die tomorrow."

"Lady Essia of Tovias, owner of the only brothel this side of the mountains. Only fool brave enough to skirt the law right here in plain sight of the King, much less in front of the Order." When she opened her mouth, Bredych shushed her. "Back when you were on the streets, she came after you. She had *plans* for you. I knew she was bad news, Shen, but I didn't know everything until...."

Until the job. It'd been right there in front of her...

❦

BREDYCH AND SHENDRA GATHERED AT A SMALL TABLE WHERE parchment after parchment lay strewn across its wood. Across from them sat their master, his fingers dancing across the table as he spoke. "Shendra, your first target is Lady Essia of Tovias. This job comes directly from the King, so ready or not, your initiation into the Order happens in three days' time."

"Can I ask what her crime was?" She knew, but she needed him to say it out loud.

Elish tilted his head to study her face a moment before replying. "We will always tell you your mark's crime against the Thirteen. For one to deliver Justice, one must understand why it is necessary. While the Lady runs a brothel, her real money comes from the buying and selling of women."

"That's not legal," said Shendra, earning herself a glare.

"That would be why the King has ordered her killed, unofficially of course," said her brother.

Shendra bit her tongue. Killing was against the Thirteen as well, whether or not it was for Justice. Not that the Order would ever see the irony.

"Lady Essia's sneaky. She preys on those vulnerable, those too poor to do naught else but sell themselves for half a penny." When the master's eyes fell upon her, she felt smaller than a rain droplet. "Girls like you once were."

Master Elish slid a small scrap of parchment across the table toward Bredych, whose face paled when he read it. She leaned towards him, and he crumpled the parchment into his fist before she could see what was written upon it. "We had our eyes on you from the moment your mother died."

Her heart cried in protest at her Master's words. Bredych had said coming after her had been his idea… Was it another lie to keep her where they wanted her?

"Even still, Lady Essia almost reached you first. Another day and you would've been another girl gone missing."

"I still say Shendra would have seen through the Lady's lies," said Bredych, but Shendra shook her head.

"That time on the streets—between the sharp pains in m'belly and the cold ache at night, I would've agreed to near anythin' iffen it meant a solid meal and a warm bed."

"Which is what the Lady counts on." Master Elish shuffled through the stack of parchments before he continued. "It's not as if she would have told you what you'd be doing at the brothel. Nor would she have exposed you to it immediately. Our Lady Essia is smart. Sly even."

The writing across the pages blurred slightly. "Let me guess—she'd rattle off some promise of food and a bed in exchange for some housekeepin' maybe. Like dishes at her inn or somethin' simple. Get a good month's time in with that warm bed and good meal, and then I'd-a-owed her."

"Exactly. You would have been in her debt. She would have been well within her right to take it out of you or have you hauled up before the local constable if you didn't make it right. Of course, she'd lie about how much you owed and the laws that backed her. What's a starving kid like you going to know about the law?"

Bredych stood, his lithe frame pacing between the chairs and the wall. Every time he passed her, his foot knocked against the leg of her chair. Whether accidental or intentional, the repetition made her eye twitch. She didn't blame him. They both shared a healthy imagination. Not that they needed one after the Master read the parchments. The Order and the King had ten years' of history on Lady Essia's. "So how does she sell folks? I imagine that's much harder to sneak by the Boahim Senate," asked Bredych.

Another question danced on the tip of Shendra's tongue, but she held her peace. This one would wait another breath or three.

Master Elish ran a hand across his bald head before he answered. "That question had us stumped for a decade. We could have killed Lady Essia a dozen times by now, but we'd still be left with too many questions and a possible slave trade out there. Our informants know she tends to sell those who give her grief or those who are too old or broken for her brothel. Ships come from across the Harren Sea, so she's trading with people outside of Boahim."

The idea that continents other than Boahim existed still spun Shendra's young head. The Order's library held more books than her mind had been able to imagine as a child. "You believe yourself capable of your task, which you are, but you must be careful. She spins words with a poison stronger than those you've studied," said Master Elish.

"Master, I get why this Lady Essia's a danger, but twice you've given me information that's raised questions in my mind."

"Such as?"

"For one, why were ya watchin' me after our mother died? I can understand my brother watchin' me, but why the Order?"

"And...?"

She ran her tongue over lips too dry. "And why do ya think she'll be able to get her hooks into me? There's somethin' ya ain't sayin'—somethin' on that parchment ya been worryin' on for the past twenty minutes."

Their master's fingers paused at the page's edge. Beside him, one candle flickered and died as the wick drowned in wax. Master Elish poured the excess into the bucket beneath the table and used another candle to relight the wick. "When your father died, your mother had little to support herself on, much less her children. A year after his passing, your mother was set to meet with Lady Essia—"

Bredych ceased pacing, his hand still curled into fists.

"Your mother made an appointment—though we don't know what the end result would have been. Before her engagement, she met with us." Her brother bit off a curse as their Master continued. "She needed money, and we needed someone who could get inside and feed us needed information. Everyone we sent in from outside was too suspect, no matter how good their training. Your mother already had a connection with Lady Essia. She had access we did not."

"Ya used her, and it got her killed." When Shendra spoke the words, she thought her brother would leap out of his skin. Instead, he resumed his pacing. The kicks to her chair were harder now. Hard enough to bounce her in her seat.

Master Elish frowned. "You're mother's death was unfortunate."

The candle's flame shook when Bredych's fist hit the table. "You set'er up to die and call it 'unfortunate'?" Bredych's sharp laughter left bumps across her arms that danced in rhythm to the candle's flame.

"It was a poor choice of words. Regardless, your anger marks you unready to lead the Amaskans. Jobs must serve Justice, not vengeance. No one would blame you, Bredych, for needing some time."

"I'm ready, if for no other reason than to keep you from it." Her brother's shadow framed the wall for a moment before he strode from the room.

How long had he known the truth about their mother's death? Had he known when he'd rescued Shendra from the streets? Beneath the table, her legs shook.

"Now do you understand why the Lady must be brought to Justice?"

Shendra nodded automatically. The Lady had killed her mother, so why couldn't she bring herself to kill the woman? Was it cowardice or something else?

Master Elish picked up the crumpled parchment and spread it out across the table in front of her. The candlelight flickered as he left through the single door, and her fingers trembled as she brought the page within view. The familiar handwriting slanted heavier than usual, its tiny print bearing smudges from the butt of her palm.

*If yer readin' this, I've failed in findin' what this Order wanted me to. They swore they'd look after ya both, but they'd tell me anythin' ta serve their own purpose. These folks're sneakier than the rain down a sewer grate, and all for their precious justice. If your father're still alive, so many things would be different.*

*I needed the money—I ain't gonna lie to ya. I was all set to sellin' whatever I had to with Lady Essia when them Order folks found me. Like them stories yer father always told, I was a spy for 'em. That Lady be pure evil if ever evil existed. The things she made them girls do. Ya must stay away from 'er at all costs. When she found me out, she nabbed some of my hair when I was sleepin'. I know it 'cause she told me so when I woke the next morn'.*

*Rolled over and there she was, just a starin' at me all wicked like. I didn't peg 'er for a mystic or nothin', but I wonder. She said she'd a secret, and if I wanted to live, I'd keep her secrets like she kept mine.*

*I told them Order folks what I saw her doin', and then I wrote this for the both of ya. They told me they'd give this note to ya once Shendra was older, and I'm hopin' they've done what they said. Shendra, ya must look so grown up by now. I wish I could see it. Whatever you do, don't go trustin' these weasels. While I knew what I was gettin' into, I can imagine you musta lived a hard life without me and your Da. I've seen plenty enough street rats to know the life that leads to, but I hope you've found somethin' better. Somethin' learned.*

*Shendra, ya know your brother. He'll look after ya and all, but his temper's gonna get him into trouble. Take care of him. Remind him of the good in life. Remind him of me.*

The page had landed on the table, its corner touching the candle's flame. Shendra had swatted at the flame until it died, leaving a black charred corner behind. She'd folded the paper and shoved it into her pocket. *Why did Master Elish show me this?* Her resolve to join the Order wanted to flee with the rest of her, even more so now that she'd read her mother's letter.

Fewer than seven hours remained until they left for the job, and her mind was anything but clear. Bredych's carefree smile held no hint of the man who'd stormed out of the meeting room a few days before. Her wounded finger caressed the paper. "Bredych?"

"Hmm?"

"Are ya sure about this? 'Bout my joinin' the Order? I know it's what you've wanted to do since Da...but me? I don't know. Fightin' is fine, but killin'?" Her brother nodded, and she asked, "Even if they're the reason Ma died?"

"Especially if they're the reason."

She shivered at the blankness in his eyes.

A day's journey by horseback. That was all that lay between Shendra and her mission. That and a good night's sleep. For all that her body begged for rest, Shendra's mind spun circles around her worry. When the knock on her door repeated itself, her eyes gave up in their attempt to stay shut. She held her sword before her—even here. Especially here.

The door remained silent as she cracked it open. Bredych stood outside, his hood drawn up. "Couldn't sleep. Figured we might as well set out for Tovias."

She opened the door wide enough to allow him entrance before closing and locking it. He laughed, and when she turned away from the door, he held her already packed bag. "Trouble sleeping, too?"

"Of course. I think anyone would the night before they murder someone, evil or not."

"It's not murder. It's Justice."

Shendra frowned as she tucked her socked feet into black riding boots. Unable to sleep, she'd bathed and dressed for travel in the gear of a typical sword-for-hire, something to blend in with other folks heading to the city of Tovias. After dressing, she'd lay in bed until the pre-dawn hours and waited. Waited for her future, for a murder that would stain her. She'd shivered in the cold of her thoughts until his knock.

Bredych sat across the foot of her bed, pointedly not watching as she donned her leather armor. Simple stuff, but when it came time, she'd shuck it off anyway. All it would do was weigh her down. Her fingers shook as she strapped her tabard to her belt.

The hood of her cloak would cover her face in the early morning. Not that she had a scar to hide—not yet. Not ever if she failed her test.

As if he read her thoughts, her brother rubbed his jaw where it met his ear. "Does the mark hurt?" she asked, as she stared at the circle marring his skin.

"A bit. Like a cat scratch."

Fully dressed, Bredych carried both their bags to the stables where a trainee curled up in the corner, a book in his lap. A few battle-steeds neighed as they passed. Her brother had dreamed of the mark, whereas horses traveled in and out of her dreams. Shendra's gaze lingered on the battle-steeds. The kindness in their eyes failed to match the muscular-bulk of their bodies. One beast rolled his eyes at her while another sniffed her outstretched fingers with anticipation. Finding nothing to eat, he backed into his stall with a sigh.

"Better not let Master Elish catch you doing that."

She shoved her hands in her pockets. Her brother Bredych, upholder of rules.

Towards the end of a long line of battle steeds lay several dozen regular horses used for travel. They saddled two and tied their single bags into place before exiting the massive stables through the rear. Those on guard duty nodded them out as their horses matched pace. The barest hints of flesh-color breached the horizon, and Shendra tugged her cloak tighter across her shoulders. Neither of them spoke until well after the sun rose. They hugged the ragged coastline, and Shendra flinched each time a gull cried out as it dove in and out of the surf for its morning meal.

"You're on edge."

She sighed as her fingers touched the note in her pocket.

Bredych must've seen the motion as his hand shot out only to stop three inches from her nose. "Give it here."

"Give what?"

"The paper in your pocket. It's the note Master Elish had, isn't it?"

Shendra shifted her weight in the saddle. When he gesticulated again, she handed the note over with a sigh. "Ya said ya didn't know 'til Master Elish gave us the job."

Her brother nodded but remained silent.

"Yer angry."

His horse picked up its speed, and she urged hers to keep pace.

"Now yer almost happy to watch me turn my life upside down."

"Did it ever dawn on you that maybe I want the Lady dead? That maybe she deserves to die for what she's done?"

The vengeance poured out of him, and he kicked his horse forward into a gallop. The dirt road beneath her horse's hooves shifted. Rocks stuck out from the dirt as they approached the coast, and she slowed her horse as he picked his way around the rough edges. Bredych never slowed, his horse barreling through the salty air like one of the Thirteen rode his tail, and she lost sight of him for a while.

Half an hour later, she caught a glimpse of a hooded figure on the roadside. When she stopped alongside her brother, he tossed a pebble at her.

"What happened to yer horse?"

"Damn thing bucked me and took off down that-a-way." He thrust his arm in the direction of a small trail leading away from the cliff edge.

"How long ago?"

Bredych's eyebrows tried to cross each other as he scowled. "Long enough that he's long gone."

"I'm bettin' he found a nice stream to drink from and is sittin' nearby. Think ya can stay outta trouble while I take a looksee?"

He waved a hand at her, and she turned her horse off on the smaller trail. Branches knocked into the horse's flank as they passed through heavy brush, so she allowed her mount to find his own speed through the roughage. She'd traveled maybe ten minutes when she caught the gurgling sound of a stream. Another two minutes found fresh horse droppings and then the stream itself.

Light hoofprints to the left and right confused her. She dismounted and tied her reins to a nearby tree before heading left. As she drew closer to the river, the prints shifted from dusty hoof prints to prints that marred the growin' mud below. The prints were deep enough to leave little pools of water within them as they led to the water's edge before disappearing. The prints were too deep; the horse was carrying a rider.

She traced the prints back to her horse and followed the second set that veered to the right. These remained light all the way to the edge where Bredych's horse stood head down, munching on a patch of green clover. For all that he appeared calm, his ears followed her every movement. "Steady," she whispered as she approached.

The horse continued eating though his ears followed her movements. Several birds took to the sky as she touched the reins, and the horse raised his head in alarm. Shendra scanned the river for signs of company, but the trees shadowed too much and not enough all at once. After a quick glance around, she led the horse back to her own.

The way the silence settled around the trees unnerved her, and after tying his horse's reins to her saddle, she mounted her horse with more urgency than expected. The beast whinnied in protest and set off at a quickened pace through the brush. When she broke through the thicket near the road, her brother was gone.

"Dammit. Dammit. Dammit."

Only one set of footprints led towards the road meaning no one kidnapped him. By the track marks, no one had tossed him over someone's horse either. She kicked her horse forward, following his boot prints.

*When I find him, I'm gonna kill 'im.*

Shendra's temper grew short as the day grew long, and without a target, she ground her teeth until she thought they'd break. The trail pulled away from the cliff, and the brush thickened. When her brother leapt out of a bit of bramble, her horse reared. "Dammit, Bredych, what—"

"Shhhhh," he hissed. "Quick, pull the horses into the brush."

"What—"

His eyes widened, and she slid from the saddle in a rush. Something bellowed behind her, and she tugged at the reins. Both horses balked, the whites of their eyes contrasting their black coats. "If they were battle-steeds, I wouldn't be wrestlin' them," she muttered.

Bredych's fingers scrambled at his saddlebag. "Leave the horses. Grab your pack."

"How're we gonna get to Tovias without the horses?" Another crash through the brush left her tugging at the strings of her bag. They weren't gonna make it to Tovias, not with whatever approached them. She pulled her bag free as her horse reared.

Shendra rolled away from the hooves and into a bush, her shoulder striking a rock in the dirt. Despite the sharp pain, she remained still as something large and angry sent their horses off in opposite directions.

Dust filled her lungs far in advance of the wagon, which rolled by much too slowly for Shendra's tastes. Its wheels stopped in front of the brush where they hid, and from behind the wagon came a rumble like table legs dragged across stone.

The long snout sniffed the air, and beside her, Bredych's hand clenched her cloak. "What's that?" she whispered.

He held a finger to her mouth and then pointed. Two ears twitched in their direction. Like a stable cat, the creature bore lithe, springy muscles and the usual set of four appendages, but unlike any cat she'd seen, its wide eyes bore an eerie intelligence almost magical in nature.

The cloaked figure in the wagon's front seat muttered something, and the creature nodded once before it turned its head in their direction. Shendra held her breath as it met her gaze and growled.

When Bredych's cold fingers touched hers, she bit her tongue to keep from shouting. He squeezed her hand as the creature smiled, all sharp teeth and forked crimson tongues. Before it stepped in their direction, the cloaked figure snapped its fingers and set the wagon to moving. Irritation flared in the creature's eyes as the wagon moved past their hiding place.

A full ten minutes passed before either one of them dared speak and longer until they did so above a whisper. "What in the Thirteen was that?" she asked.

"A *chathula*. A creature of myth as far as the Order's library is concerned. The last time one was spotted was back when the Little Dozen Kingdoms were still Boahim."

"What's one doin' here? And who was the cloaked figure?"

Bredych shook his head, though his haunted gaze remained fixed on the road ahead of them—the only road to Tovias, now blocked by a creature of unknown intelligence.

Shendra pulled her cloak tighter across her shoulders. "Does this change the job? I mean, do we keep goin' or should we report back to Master Elish?"

"If we lose this opportunity to take out Lady Essia, we might not get another chance. Her honor guard will be preoccupied tonight, so this is it. Besides, the orders come from the King. I don't want to be the one to explain to His Highness why we failed to follow his orders, do you? Come on."

She followed him from the brush and out onto the open road. The visibility made her skin crawl as she walked alongside her brother in silence. Both flinched when a small tree branch fell beside the dirt road, and when they glanced up, two squirrels chased each other through the canopy.

An hour passed before signs of a settlement cropped up, and as they approached the lone woodcutter's house, they kept to the shadows until they were sure no one was home. The wagon's tracks led on past the house, and Bredych kept watch as Shendra checked the nearby barn.

One empty stall greeted her, and one held a young gelding who snorted at her presence. When she held out an apple from her pack, he accepted the offering and munched greedily on it while she tossed a riding blanket across his back. A quick search gave her no saddle, though reins, bridle, and a bit lay nearby.

In search of another apple, the gelding accepted the bit, then whinnied when he found it tasting of leather rather than juicy sweet. She dug a few coins out of the small pouch at her hip and left them in the horse's stall. She might be a killer, but she was no thief.

She led the horse outside and up the road where her brother waited. "Looks like we'll be ridin' double."

"Ugh, and bareback as well. No saddle?"

"Owner's got two mounts, and the other was missin'. They might've ridden to town on the other and taken the saddle. At least this'll be faster than walkin' to Tovias."

Bredych mounted first, and the horse flattened his ears for a moment before settling into his new role. "We'll have to go slow enough to stay behind that wagon. Last thing we need is to gain the attention of whoever or whatever's traveling toward Tovias," he said as Shendra hopped up behind him.

Arms wrapped around her brother, she listened to the birds overhead as they rode to Tovias and closer to the mark.

*And closer to my life changing forever.*

They stopped several times—both to give their horse a break and to ensure they didn't overtake the wagon somewhere ahead—and as the sun grew closer to the horizon, the trees thinned and farms sprung up alongside the road. Dressed as hired hands, neither of them hid as they traveled, though once they stopped when a farmer offered them some day-old bread.

"Figgered ya need it, bein' on hard times and all," he'd said with a frown.

It wasn't until they'd neared Tovias that Shendra realized what the farmer had meant, and she chuckled.

"Something funny?"

"We're gonna ride into town lookin' like the world's worst fighters —us sharin' a horse with no saddle and a young mount at that. Two light bags 'tween us, and they're like to think us on the run."

Bredych slowed their mount with a curse. "That will set too many eyes on us. We'll have to ditch the mount and approach on foot. Least that way we look more like the fighters we're supposed to be."

This time Shendra cursed. She should've thought of that as it was on her to strategize the optimal ways in and out of the location.

After she dismounted, he followed and gave the horse their last apple. As the gelding munched on it, Bredych placed his hand on Shendra's shoulder. "Hey, you're not going to think of everything. Not the first time out anyway."

"But an Amaskan can't make mistakes like that. It's how you end up dead."

"True, but this is why you aren't alone this time. You won't be sent on a solo job for a good year or two. There's still plenty for you to learn before that happens," he said as they followed the wagon's trail toward the wall.

A guardsman held up his hand at their approach. "Names and purpose of visit." Their cover story as two swords-for-hire looking for work had him nodding as he scribbled something down on a piece of parchment before waving them through the gate. Shendra remained silent as the city of Tovias rose up to greet her.

From the way the buildings' ruddy brick didn't crumble to the cobbled road leading through the town's center, traces of wealth wove its way across Tovias. Even with the sun setting, the tallest building stood out as the grand center of activity with three stories and balconies wrapping around three of its four sides. Women and men of varying ages and states of dress draped themselves across the railing as they waved to passers-by.

Rather than follow the cobble street towards the Lady's establishment, Shendra steered them towards the local Guild where a burly man sporting a bushy, red mustache stood. "Welcome to the Mercenary Guild. Fair work for fair pay. What can I do to help you?" he asked.

She fetched the scrap of parchment carrying the Guild's crest and handed it to the man. It listed their fake identities, which the burly man read over while shifting his gaze between the parchment and their leather armor. They wore nothing fancy, but the armor carried enough nicks to speak of the action they'd seen.

He handed the parchment back with a frown. "We're rather short on jobs in Tovias. Is there something specific you're looking for?"

"We're passin' through on our way to the capital. Perhaps ya could give us the name of a decent inn?"

The man relaxed at her question. "The *Two Fish Inn* is just down the road. Nothin' special, but the beds are comfortable and Sally'll treat you right."

"Our thanks," said Bredych, and they turned away from the Guild.

Once out of earshot, Shendra said, "He really didn't wanna give us work."

Bredych nodded. "Perhaps with Lady Essia all but in charge, they stick to their own. Something to report back to the Guild."

"If we were Guild members perhaps." Shendra snorted. "What do I care if he's crooked?"

Up ahead lay the inn, a good six buildings away from Lady Essia's. It was rough in comparison. No brick lay out of place, but the sign out front carried a touch more sun fading, and the front door lacked a fresh coat of paint.

"You never know when you might need this identity or the Guild again. Everything that concerns your merc persona concerns you." Her cheeks grew warm at his chastisement, and he raised his voice as they neared the inn and said, "So glad the Guild could recommend a good place."

The bar matron who ran the place lacked a fresh coat of paint as well. Her blouse bore multiple stains, and her oily hair was tied back at her nape with a jagged scrap of leather. No smile greeted them as they entered the tavern on the first floor, though Sally did nod in their direction, and when Shendra reached the bar, the bar matron pointed to a sign overhead.

One notch a night was more than most inns, but in a town like Tovias, everything was bound to cost more as the city served as a main thoroughfare for those traveling to the capital of Sadai. Without complaint, Shendra removed the necessary coinage from her bag and placed it on the counter.

"Just the one night?" asked Sally.

"Hopin' to find work that'll have us travelin' on rather quickly. Iffen we need another night, will that be a problem?"

Sally shook her head. "Long as you pay, I'll find ya a spot. Might be on the tavern floor, but I'll find ya a place. Take the last room on the left."

Shendra took the offered key and set off towards the stairs at a pace that spoke of too long in the saddle and not enough rest. Once behind closed doors, she dropped the facade and turned her attention to the room.

"You lucked out," said Bredych as he pointed at the room's lone window. "First plan it is then."

While Bredych rattled on, she paced the room. One bed in the corner was easier to defend, and yes, the lone window would allow them to exit the inn without being seen, but something about the room set Shendra on edge. When she neared the window, the street below was well-occupied at this time of the evening, but what would it look like come midnight?

"Did ya notice the torch lights outside?" she asked, and her brother paused, small travel bag still in his grasp. "Plan one has a complication if this street remains busy and lit."

"Nothing we can't handle." Bredych dropped his bag on the floor before stretching out across the bed. "Wake me up in a few hours if you need some rest."

As his eyes closed, she dragged a raggedy chair over to the window where she took a seat to wait. Typical Bredych—complete relaxation in the face of danger. Shendra frowned as she watched the Lady's establishment across the road. Only a few men entered through the front doors while the rest scuttled by, heads downcast as they passed.

Two hours burned away before the women on the balconies retreated indoors, and another hour before the street below quieted. Several torches remained burning, and when she cracked open the window, their oily stench wafted up to her.

Once the moon was high in the sky, a young man on stilts lumbered from torch to torch where he stamped out most of the flames. The street fell dark. Shadows moved in the windows of Lady Essia's as upstairs guests were "made comfortable" and downstairs guests were served an assortment of liquor and conversation.

Shendra closed the curtains to their room before returning to her travel bag. While her brother slept, she shed her hired-hand outfit for the form-fitting clothes of the Order, black fabric that covered the skin, yet breathed and stretched as she moved. Black sleeves and leggings ended in tapered silk, and she pulled on toed shoes and fingerless gloves next. She bound the ends tightly at her wrists and ankles and wound another wrap about her waist and face, leaving only her eyes visible.

She left the jar of grease beside her shed clothing and nudged her brother with her foot. When he woke, he nodded once in complete silence before fetching his own clothing. More practiced than she, he donned his wraps quickly while she peeked through the window.

He indicated his readiness by placing the grease jar on the window ledge. Eyelids and fingernails were covered in the black concoction, though not the fingertips. Not if they wanted to survive the night.

Shendra listened at the window and hearing nothing, leaned her head outside. No one passed by on the streets.

It was time.

Being her trial, it was up to her to lead the mission, and with that, she swung one leg and then the other over the window ledge. The rooftop, while well-shingled, was slick enough in the summer humidity that she crept across it with care until she reached the other side. Shadowed and silent, this side of the building almost touched the building next door's rooftop, and she stepped across the gap with ease. Her gaze flickered between the roof and the street below, and behind her, she was sure her brother did the same. Four rooftops later, the space between buildings stretched further than two horses head to tail, and Shendra paused.

"What is it?" Bredych whispered.

When she pointed at the gap, he took a few steps back before running toward the edge. Shendra winced at the thump as he landed, then slid to a stop safely on Lady Essia's roof. *Showoff*, she mouthed, and like a child, he stuck his tongue out.

Her leap across the space was both quieter and more elegant as she rolled on her toes to keep from sliding, yet she crouched as low to the roof as she could, a motion echoed by her brother as they waited several heartbeats. No one in the closest room moved, at least not in their direction, as the room's occupants continued their rhythmic dance between the sheets. Shendra gestured for Bredych to follow her as she slipped beneath that window and then a second one. The third window held no flickering candlelight, and she poked her head above the ledge.

Nothing moved from within the room. When she crawled through the opening, the floor chilled her slippered feet, and she suppressed a shudder. Her breath clouded the air before her, and with a frown, she glanced over her shoulder.

Bredych sat on the window ledge, one foot posed to touch the floor and the other a mere six inches from the wood surface. His face, a frozen mix of concentration and shock, didn't move, nor did his chest rise and fall with the motion of breathing.

Rather than run toward him, Shendra remained still as the hair on her arms stood on end. Someone or some*thing* was in the room with them. A slight hiss sounded to her left, followed by a familiar long snout as the *chathula* slinked into view. The creature stopped a few inches from her brother, a sound escaping it that was half-laugh, half-hiss.

Fear kept her rooted in place. Probably a boon as she would've giggled at the idea of a laughing cat. It turned to face her, intelligence and a hint of malice in its slitted eyes.

"Breaking into the Lady's home. *Tsk-tsk.*"

Her mouth grew dry in one heartbeat. One thing to have a laughing cat, but quite another to have a talking one.

"The Lady would *rrr*eward me with fresh fish if I brought her your hea*rrr*ts."

The way its *r*'s rolled further added to the *chathula's* oddness, and Shendra held up her hands. "I-Is my brother still alive?" she asked.

Another laugh escaped a wry, toothy grin. "For the moment."

"How is he...still?"

"My magic holds him in stasis. It's a helpful way to stop one's prey from escaping."

At the word, Shendra's skin prickled. Magic was old, something written about in hidden myths and legends. Only the Thirteen possessed powers, and they were gods, not cats. "Are ya a god?" she whispered.

"No, what I am is hungry."

The *chathula* paced between the siblings, its whiskers twitching as it licked its mouth. If Shendra could force the cat to the right, all she need do is knock her brother backwards through the window. It wouldn't be their first eight-foot fall off a roof. Either way, it was loads better than remaining inside with the cat. As if the creature knew her thoughts, it stepped between them and sat on its haunches in a rather cat-like manner.

Shendra held up her hands in front of her. "If yer hungry, perhaps we can help. Does the Lady feed ya fish? There's fresh fish comin' through Sadai's ports on the daily. We could arrange for ya to—"

"Magic doesn't require fish but blood."

"I didn't ask 'bout magic but about *you*. What does a great *chathula* like yerself desire?"

Its crimson tongues flicked out where they froze in place, forgotten. "It *has* been a while since we tasted fish…"

"If ya let us go, I'll bring ya the freshest fish you've ever tasted."

The creature shook its head. "*He* stays here. You can retrieve the fish."

For a moment, Shendra hesitated, and the creature's eyes narrowed as long claws tapped the wooden floor by Bredych's feet. "Ya won't harm him while I'm gone?"

"I am a being of my word."

She gave her brother one last look before squeezing between him and the window. Once on the rooftop, the overwhelming urge to flee the city of Tovias left a sour taste in her mouth. *Since when would the unknown have me willin' to leave my brother behind?*

Her trembling legs left her sliding more than climbing down the roof, and she landed on the dirt below with an *oomph* and a roll. A quick glance told her no one was outside to have seen her fall, let alone heard her, but she tucked herself into the shadows cast by the tall building just in case. While Tovias wasn't a port town, it lay close enough to the *Harren Sea* that salt and brine pierced the air when the wind blew. The local fishmonger was bound to have something fresh enough to please the cat-like creature holding her brother hostage.

Of course, at this hour, everything but Lady Essia's was closed.

Shendra crept through the shadowed streets until at the town's edge, she located what she sought. No fishy smell caught her nose—only the slight smell of sea water that drifted from beneath the shack's door. The exterior displays were empty of anything worth stealing, and the overhang covered whatever rested in the window sills. The door knob, a simple thing of bronze, was locked to the touch, and she glanced over her shoulder once before retrieving her lock pick rod from a small pouch at her waist.

It'd been intended to pick the lock to Lady Essia's room, but instead, she extended the thin, metal rod into the lock, notches facing up. She pushed it upward and listened. When the spring failed to compress, she pulled the rod out a smidge and repeated the procedure until the door unlocked. Shendra hesitated before entering, her ears alert for the sounds of someone moving. Silence was her only answer, and she slid inside, careful to place her feet gently. The trickle of street light left little to see by, though it glinted off a metal handle ten feet ahead.

Hands stretched out in front of her, she moved past a few barrels toward the tiny shack's rear and stopped when she spotted glinting metal which proved to be a handle. She gave it a good tug, and the wooden door opened, exposing a small hole in the ground. Even with the summer heat, the ground kept the water cool enough that she winced when her fingers reached into the darkness. Something slick brushed past her fingers, then another as she grabbed hold of it.

How many fish would a *chathula* want to eat? To be on the safe side, she fetched six from the stock below ground. Without twine to keep them together, she slid them tail-side-up along her lock pick rod with a frown. Seemed a waste of a good tool, but with no other choice, she set back in the direction of Lady Essia's, her fish rod resting across her shoulder.

One of the Lady's women stood out front, and Shendra sidled along the building's left side until she stood below her brother half-frozen in the window. She couldn't climb with the rod outstretched, but even without it, there were no crates or trees with which to pull herself up to the roof. Not even a trellis leaned against the building—almost as if the Lady had thought of the dangers of an exposed, open window. "*Pssst,* kitty?" she whispered, then flinched as a large shadow crossed overhead.

In the dark, the *chathula's* frame made a much more imposing figure as it leapt down from the rooftop, its canines visible as steel-like glints. Its nostrils flared as its head bobbed in her direction. "I smell fish," it purred.

She'd barely moved the rod before the creature was on it, purrs and snarls punctuated by ripping flesh. All six were devoured in a matter of a few breaths, and once done, the *chathula* used a paw the size of her head to clean its muzzle. A dozen or more heartbeats passed before Shendra cleared her throat. "Will ya please release my brother?"

Its gaze shifted from relaxed to alert as it turned to face her. "What is your business with the Lady?"

The lie stuck to her tongue, and when Shendra opened her mouth, the truth flowed too easily. "Lady Essia's no lady. She deals with the buyin' and sellin' of girls. We've been sent here to ensure that stops. How did ya do that?"

"Do what?"

"Force me to tell the truth."

The *chathula* shrugged. "It's a side-effect of my magic. My travel companion came here to purchase women for his homeland across the giant sea. Why is this a concern of yours?"

Shendra stiffened. "It's wrong to sell people. People have the right to be free, as the Thirteen have declared. Surely a creature like you would understand."

Rank like death, its breath warmed her face as the creature moved closer. "What would I understand of the ways of humans? It is not my caring what they do with each other."

"And if someone were to steal yer cubs and sell 'em to someone? What then?"

Its eyes shifted almost silver in the small light trickling from Lady Essia's. One paw lifted, its sharp claws extended in Shendra's direction, and she held her breath as one claw touched her jaw. No tattoo marked her flesh, not until she passed her test, yet the *chathula* drew a circle below her ear. Blood trickled down her neck, but she remained still.

"If someone dared to steal my cub, they would not live to see the sunrise, so I will mark you to remember you. Should you attempt such a foolish task, I will know you for who you are...Amaskan."

Shendra opened her mouth, but the creature placed a single claw against her lips.

"I understood the analogy, child, as I have lived much longer than you humans do. I'll not stop whatever deed you have planned, but know that if we should meet again, I'll not hesitate to do what my companion wishes while the Lady plays, as my debt to him is great."

In the moment it took to inhale, the *chathula* disappeared in the shadows. Above her, Bredych stumbled in the window as his body unfroze.

"*Psst*," she hissed and backed up against the next building. When he caught sight of her on the ground, he retreated from the window to the roof's ledge. Without a word, he held his arm over the side to pull her onto the roof.

The action was louder than the way they'd first come, but the only movement this late came from within the building. This time, their entrance into the bedroom was uninhibited. Bredych stopped near a bed covered in fur, his jaw clenched. "You wanna explain to me what happened a moment ago?" he whispered.

"When a creature that shouldn't exist used magic to freeze ya?"

He nodded. "Where's the creature now? Does its corpse lay in the alley or did you find somewhere to hide it?"

"The *chathula* and I made a deal. I fed it fish, and it promised to ignore our task tonight." When her brother bit back a curse, she frowned. "What?"

"Making a deal with a magical creature is like making a deal with the Thirteen. One never sees their actual intention until it's too late. Be careful."

Bredych motioned for her to go first, and she walked to the door, only once causing the floorboards to creak beneath her feet. Shendra leaned her ear against the wood and listened for sounds of movement on the other side. Somewhere nearby, several people moaned as passion held them together, but otherwise, no one paced the hall. "I thought Lady Essia enjoyed listenin' to the house's clients," she said.

"She does."

"Well, she doesn't today. There ain't no one out there pacin' around."

"Something isn't right. If she's not pacing the hallway, where is she? The *chathula* must have told her we were here."

Shendra shook her head and opened the door a crack. Light streamed into the bedroom, and she paused to give her eyes a moment to adjust. As she'd determined, no one stood in the hallway. The sounds from the room next-door rose in volume, and a few other cries from a second room joined the nightly orchestra.

Rather than wait for her brother to complain again, she opened the door completely and winced when it squeaked. Beside her, Bredych pointed at the door hinge. It was too late now to grease it, but she did so anyway so he couldn't report the mistake.

Small oil lanterns whose smoke left the faint odor of fish in the air lit the empty hallway. Every bit of information the Order had gathered suggested this was never the case, and the hair on Shendra's arms rose. She took a deep breath to suppress her body's reaction, then stepped outside the bedroom.

Three doors down would be Lady Essia's quarters, and this time, Shendra remembered to grease the door's hinges before she tested the knob. Surprisingly, it was unlocked, and the open door exposed a stylish room of furs and brightly woven rugs. Lit candles burned on the room's few tables, giving them full view. Multiple chairs were scattered about, some empty and others covered in cast-off clothing. Several blankets hung over the bed in the room's corner, and sticking out from beneath them was a pair of tall boots.

Shendra pointed at them, and her brother nodded. "Hers by the heels," he whispered in her ear.

A curtain separated the room from a bathing chamber, and she stopped before it. No steam brushed her face, nor did the sound of dripping water touch her ears. Shendra withdrew her dagger from its sheath at her waist and used it to separate the thick cotton, exposing a metal tub, which was dry to the touch. More candles burned on two short tables, and a stool held a throw pillow that matched two on the tile floor.

When she gestured for them to leave the room, Bredych shook his head and pointed at a couch. He wanted to hide and wait, that much was apparent, but something about the way the *chathula* had spoken made her think the Lady had something else in mind for the evening.

There were eight rooms total on the second floor, one of them being Lady Essia's quarters. A second was a shared bathing chamber, while the others were rooms used to "entertain" guests. A bar took up most of the first floor, while the building's rear served as both the Lady's office and place of auction. *If she ain't pacin' the halls upstairs, she should be in her quarters. With those empty, maybe she's somewhere else upstairs?* The creature had mentioned Lady Essia playing...

Rather than wait, Shendra went door to door with her ear pressed hard against the wood. The first voice was too young, as was the second. The third room lay silent, like the room they'd entered, leaving two remaining rooms to check. Outside the first, she paused as two women whispered inside. Neither voice sounded particularly aged, not that she'd recently heard Lady Essia's voice. Someone tapped her shoulder, a rapid succession of three taps, and despite recognizing the code as her brother, Shendra bit her lip to keep from screaming.

His look clearly read: *How did I startle you?*

When she remained silent, he pointed at the last remaining door and arched a brow. She nodded before ambling over and pressing her ear against the wood. On the other side was a deep voiced man and a deeper voiced woman, both at the end of a much more interesting night than Shendra was having, and she pulled her ear away from the door.

She gestured for Bredych to follow her back to Lady Essia's quarters and once behind the closed door, she whispered, "We'll wait here for her to return."

"Was she in the room?"

When she nodded, Bredych asked, "What did you hear?"

"Seems our Lady of the House has a plaything with her in the room."

His shoulder muscles tensed as he squeezed his hands into fists.

"Calm down. This was a plaything of the adult variety. Best place to hide would be her bathin' room. She'll be headin' there after I would think."

There was enough room for them both to hide if one crouched behind the thick curtains at the window and the other hid by the curtained door frame. Either way, they'd hear Lady Essia entering her room with enough time to move into place. With that in mind, Shendra claimed a nearby stool, while her brother lowered himself to a crushed velvet floor cushion. Despite her words, his muscles remained tense, and his eyes flicked to the door with every creak and shuffle they heard.

For once, Shendra relaxed into place. Their target was preoccupied, and once she retreated, with no *chathula* guarding her, they'd have her. The body trafficking would stop, and Shendra would be Amaskan.

Lost in thought, she missed her brother's movement until his fingers touched the scratch on her jaw. "What's this?" he hissed.

"The *chathula* thought it'd be funny to give me a gift as it left."

Bredych stood, his face a mix of fear and anger. "We're leaving. Now. No arguments."

He shrugged away from her grasp as he touched the bathroom

curtain. Before he could part it, the bedroom door opened, announcing Lady Essia with a light thump as it closed.

Shendra's elbow hit Bredych in the chin as he moved one way and she moved the other. Training took over as he sidestepped and positioned himself behind the door, though his eyes remained wide with fear.

*She* was supposed to be beside the doorframe.

*She* was supposed to kill Lady Essia.

Instead, she scrambled for the window curtain, tucking her feet beneath it as the bathroom door opened.

Taller than Bredych and lankier, Lady Essia swept into the bathroom wearing nothing but a sheer, silk robe in purple. She smiled a feral grin in Shendra's direction.

"If there was one place a woman should be able to be herself and be safe, it is her own home, would you not agree?" she said as she stepped closer to the window.

Long fingers gripped the curtains, and the smell of sage tickled Shendra's nose. Lady Essia stared out the window for a heartbeat before she tilted her head, her sharp blue gaze meeting Shendra's. The dagger in Shendra's fingers melted as her grip loosened its hold. When the weapon bounced off the floor, Shendra's mouth opened, but the motion made no sound.

*More magic? Is it the chathula? Did it lie to me about stayin' out of our way?*

"There. No need for weapons in this room. Not between us ladies," said Lady Essia, who flicked a finger at Shendra. "You may speak now."

Whatever held a grip on her vocal cords relaxed, and a small sigh escaped her. "How'd you—"

Lady Essia hushed her. "You're asking the wrong question, Amaskan..."

When her fingers touched Shendra's chin, a shiver ran through her like someone had struck the sensitive bone of the elbow. Behind the Lady, Bredych moved—a silent figure whose gaze stayed solely on his target. Shendra allowed her gaze to widen and roam, as if terrified, which was less feint and more truth when Lady Essia yanked Shendra's head to the side.

The Lady stared at the scratch across Shendra's jaw. "That's not a tattoo. He lied! You're no Amaskan!"

"I'm also not alone."

Bredych moved, his dirk as darkly coated as his skin. It slid between Lady Essia's shoulders, smooth as the silk she wore.

The woman froze, fingers still gripping Shendra's jaw. "Neither am I, you know." At Shendra's frown, she added, "Alone. My girls are loyal. Someone else will be Lady before my body's cold."

She faltered as she turned to face her attacker, and a droplet of blood ran from her lips. "Now this—*this* is an Amaskan."

Shendra grabbed her dagger from the floor. The way the woman stared at Bredych...

"Your girls will be free, Essia. No one will take your place," he said as he held his blade before him.

"Like you would know the taste of...freedom. You're nothing but a slave to the Order." This time, when the Lady coughed, the blood came in a rush, yet the woman remained standing. She raised a faintly glowing hand to her own chest, and when she touched it, the flesh on her back moved. Blood ceased its sprint across her robes as muscle reconnected to tendon.

Before she could think about it too long, Shendra drove her dagger into Lady Essia's hand and the blue glow flickered out. The woman screamed until Bredych's blade slashed across her throat, slicing open the skin near ear to ear.

Lady Essia crumpled to the ground, but her hands reached up, their blue glow bright enough to burn, and Bredych snapped his eyes shut in response.

"Give me yer dirk," said Shendra, and when he shoved it out before him, she seized hold of it. Tears ran down her face as she stepped around the Lady, and before the glow could blind her, she wielded the dirk like an axe, hacking at Lady Essia's hands. Sharp as the blade was, cutting through bone took more blows than expected as Shendra swung the dirk over and over again.

"You can stop now," whispered Bredych, and when she opened her stinging eyes, there was little recognizable as Lady Essia on the floor.

One hand had been completely severed, while the other hung by a few bits of skin and sinew. The Lady's face... Bile threatened to burn a hole through Shendra's throat as it raced up and out. She spun away from the gore and lost any semblance of time as she lost her dinner across the curtains.

Bredych's hand tapped her shoulder—a pattern of three. "We've got to go. Her screams have to have been heard."

"The *Chathula* swore it'd stay out of our way," she said as she wiped spittle from her mouth.

"Did it actually swear? A formal oath?"

Shendra shook her head, and he pulled her to her feet. The reek of blood followed them towards the bedroom door, and she glanced down to find crimson splattered across her clothes.

"Don't worry about it. You'll get used to it. Besides, black hides blood."

*You'll get used to it.*

Shendra choked back more bile as her brother listened at the door. He was older and wiser than she, so if he said it, it must be true. *I'll get used to it.*

"No." She pulled out of his grasp, and he frowned. "No, we can't leave without freeing the girls."

"Shendra, we can't. Not now. There are probably guards all over this place. They aren't allowed on the second floor, but sooner or later, when Lady Essia doesn't appear to give them orders, they'll ignore that rule and flood these rooms. If we're still here, we won't escape."

*I can't get used to it. I won't.*

She refused to wait for Bredych's response. The door opened easily at her touch, as did the room next-door. The man atop a young woman flushed with surprise and anger when his sport was interrupted, but her blade across his throat stopped all complaint. The girl beneath him screamed.

"The Lady's dead. Yer a slave to her, or him—" Shendra pointed at the dead man, "—no longer. Leave this place."

Bredych caught her at the next door. "Wait, if you're going to do this, at least make the kills clean and quick. Don't traumatize these poor girls with a blood bath."

"If ya think these girls ain't traumatized—"

"They are, so don't add to it!"

Shendra blinked as she hesitated. Something clicked in her brain as she craned her head to peer back at the previous room where the young woman stared blindly at the blood on her clothing. The way Shendra had.

She pushed the thought aside and barged into the second room. Seeing the girl's age, Shendra's vision narrowed, and it was all she could do to stab the burly man in the heart rather than paint the walls with his blood.

When she opened the next room, two girls stared back at her, then screamed.

"Yer free now. Leave!" shouted Shendra before she set off for the last room. This had been where Lady Essia had played host to her plaything. Bredych beat her there, but when he opened the door, no one was inside.

"Where'd he go?" asked Shendra.

"Maybe he fled when he heard all the screaming." Bredych grabbed her arm when she turned toward the stairwell. "Don't go downstairs."

"Why? There are more girls down there."

"And the ones up here can spread the word. Downstairs is a pub. There will be innocent townspeople in it. How will you tell the difference in who you're killing?"

With a growl, Shendra retreated to the room at the hall's end. She'd expected the room empty—same way it was when they'd entered —but when she opened the door, the *chathula* sat curled up in its bed.

For a moment, her body reacted, her blade out and ready to kill as it had in the previous rooms, but when the creature opened its eyes at her approach, the rage withered in her and her strength fled, leaving her to sit on the floor.

"I—I'm sorry. I forgot where I was."

The *chathula* tilted its head and sniffed the air, its whole head bobbing with the movement. "With that much blood on you, I would figure so. The window remains open should you wish to flee."

"Come," barked Bredych, but when she tried to stand, her limbs were flabby and weak. He reached beneath her armpits and hauled her up. Arm around his shoulders, he hauled her through the window and out into the cold, darkness.

"Strip."

The fresh air stirred an alertness in Shendra, and she shimmied out of her clothes while her brother did the same. Bredych laid them flat across the rooftop and rolled them into a small bunch, along with her supply pouch. A few shakes of oil from his waist flask covered the smell of blood. What they were doing went against training, but unordinary circumstances meant they had to be creative.

He motioned for her to jump down into the alley below. When he landed beside her, she was ready.

She grabbed the wads of clothing from him and lit one with the finger flint she'd pulled from her pouch. He opened his mouth, then shut it as she tossed the wads onto the rooftop. "*Chathula,* flee!" she hissed and watched as a shadow dove from the window and darted across the roof before disappearing.

"That was a fool thing to do," said Bredych as he followed her alongside the building's rear.

As smoke filled the air, it covered their retreat to the nearby inn. Unlike Lady Essia's, several storage crates sat out back, which they used to climb to the roof. Once safely inside their room, Shendra and Bredych scrubbed the gray grease from their skin. He handed her an herbal concoction that smelled like a mix of sweat and sour lemons, which they splashed on themselves to disguise the odors of smoke and blood. Both donned shirts and light breeches, then crawled into the shared straw bed.

They lay silent as sleep until the pounding on their door. When Bredych stumbled up, Shendra feigned the groggy look of one just awoken. Outside stood Sally, the bar matron, wearing a pair of slippers and a long, wrinkled tunic. "There's a fire. With the winds what they are, the roof could catch. Everyone's gonna have t'go outside."

"Sounds dangerous. Anything we can do to help?" asked Bredych.

The innkeeper peered at Shendra before looking Bredych up and down. "Yer hired hands, right? They'll be needin' strong men to haul water from the well. Iffen yer girl can pour a drink, she can help give drinks to those on break."

Shendra yawned at the insult, then stood from the bed, allowing the blanket to fall to the floor. Her shirt and breeches clung to well-defined muscles that moved like whipcord as she sought her clothing.

"My apologies, milady. Yer welcome to help the lads—"

"We'll be down shortly," said Bredych as he closed the door. After a heartbeat, he mumbled, "It's the least we could do after starting this mess."

"*We* didn't start this." Shendra shoved his breeches at him. "Lady Essia did. If we were smart, we'd be ridin' outta here. The job's done."

Mid-dress, Bredych stopped and sighed. "What's the number one rule of a job?"

"To serve Justice, always."

"And the second?"

"Don't get caught. Which is why we should leave."

Her brother shook his head. "This is why you'll be in training a good while longer. If we leave now, we look guilty. We become suspects. If we stay and help, no one looks twice at us. Why would the people who started the fire risk their lives to put it out?"

"Bad enough to kill someone, but now I gotta clean it up, too?" She smiled, but her brother ignored it. For once, his comedic self hid as the situation's seriousness loomed over them. With a shrug, Shendra tugged on sturdier breeches, followed by her boots. "What do we do with our packs?"

"Leave them. If the fire takes the inn, everything we brought can be replaced. Besides, folks serious about helping won't care about their belongings. They'll be rushing to help stop the fire."

"'Course...Sellin' girls as slaves is somethin' the honest, moral people of this town can ignore. The same moral folks who'll abandon all to save the town," she muttered. Her cheekiness stayed with her until their eventual appearance outside the inn.

Lady Essia's burned bright enough to give clear visibility across the town center, giving Shendra a glimpse of how many people stood around in bedclothes and blankets, their limbs held rooted in place by fear. Children clung to mothers as their fathers carried buckets of water towards danger. Two stories of angry red threatened nearby buildings with every gust of wind, and two buildings nearby had already succumbed to the flames' hunger.

How many people would be homeless before the night was over? How many would be hungry by winter without a home or a job to provide for their family? Shendra whispered, "I didn't mean this."

"Then help," snapped Bredych as he tugged on her arm.

At the town's well, sweaty arms thrust buckets of water towards anyone waiting. Like her brother, Shendra carried the pail where directed, then tossed the water on the flames before running back to the well for more. Her muscles enjoyed the workout, monotonous though it was, until the heat caught up with her.

Climbing through the rubble to reach flames left her skin and clothing black as coal. Still hot in most places, the remains left burns across her calves and ankles, and the overwhelming temperatures made sweat pour down her face, where the soot stung her eyes and nose.

After the last bucketful of water, she paused at a bench to catch her breath. Someone sat silently beside her, their shoulders wrapped in a torn quilt that reeked of smoke. When Shendra took a longer glance, she recognized her as one of Lady Essia's women and bolted upright.

"Don't go yet. I haven't had a chance to thank you," said the young woman.

Shendra hesitated. This woman could place her in the building before the fire and not in the inn as Bredych would have the bar matron believe.

"I know what you are. Well, what he is. You've the mark, but you've also got your hair. Do some Amaskans choose to keep their hair?"

As the young woman spoke, her voice hardened and Shendra fought the urge to run. "I don't know what yer talkin' about—"

"Please. You both were sent here to kill my mistress. It's not the first time someone's been sent to kill her, or the first time someone's been successful."

Her feet stumbled on solid ground as Shendra backed away. For all that the young woman appeared young, an age and wisdom in her eyes spoke of something else.

*How can she know of the Order's plans? And what did she mean by it not being the first time Lady Essia has died? I have to find Bredych. We need to leave.*

"If you leave now, does it count as finishing the job?"

When her fingers went to her belt, no dagger was looped there—it remained upstairs with the rest of their belongings. Rather than give away her frustration, Shendra smiled, a bright smile like she lay resting on a summer's day at the shore rather than facing the destruction of a town. "When my partner and I heard a woman was breakin' the law by indulgin' in slavery, we came to see what we'd find, is all. Plenty of young women like yerself bein' forced into pleasin' men and sold across the Harren Sea. That ain't the way of Sadai. The Thirteen have some strict rules 'bout that sorta thing."

"They do. They also have some strict rules about killing people. Or does that only apply to non-Amaskans?"

Shendra's stomach tensed in response to the question. "No, murder is against the Thirteen for everyone."

Around them, people fought a losing battle against the flames, which had spread to third and fourth buildings. When the young woman spoke again, her voice was level and calm. "My mistress may have been misunderstood, but at least she never lied to us...or herself. She took us off the streets and gave us a job, a way to make a living. I wasn't starving anymore."

The faraway look in the woman's eyes was one Shendra recognized. The ache in one's stomach without food, the desperation to soften the pangs with anything—edible or not, and the willingness to do absolutely anything to sleep somewhere soft and warm.

"She gave us an education in more than just sex. I can read and write and do sums, more than most of this town can do, and she gave me that. What did you give me? My home burned down, my mistress dead and job gone, and everything that I've ever owned in a pile of rubble. You didn't save us. You sentenced us to death."

At some point, the young woman left. Shendra never noticed as she stared at the fire in silence. Saving people...it's all she'd ever wanted to do. While killing people was technically wrong, the Order had shown her a new path to helping people. Serving the Gods by meting out Justice was a holy mission...wasn't it?

A spark hit her bare arm, and she flinched. *When did the fire move that close?* she thought as Bredych trudged over to her.

"We have to go," he said, his voice scratchy and hoarse.

"I thought we were helpin'."

"We were, but the wind's picked up. There's no stopping the fire now. We need to leave."

"No, I thought we were helpin' *them.*"

Bredych frowned. "And we did, Shendra, but unless you want to burn to death, we need to go."

She raised her head to take a better glance around her. Fire burned everywhere. Not a building was spared. She coughed in the thick smoke, and her brother pulled her to her feet.

"The townsfolk are fleeing through the front gate. The fire hasn't touched it yet. But there's a breech in the walls where the fire's been. We should take it while we can."

Shendra nodded.

Once again, her brother was pulling her to safety.

As they ran, she was fifteen again. Hungry, hurt, and wishing it would all go away.

※

THE SIDE GATE HAD ALLOWED THEM TO AVOID THE townsfolk as they fled Tovias, and when they'd arrived at a farm house outside of town, sooty and smelling of smoke, the farmer set off for the fire, leaving them in the capable hands of his wife.

Several baths and a meal later, Shendra pulled her brother aside and disclosed the conversation she'd had with the young woman, though she'd left out the part about Lady Essia possibly being alive. All that would do was kick a hornet's nest.

"Most of Sadai knows Amaskans shave their heads and bear circular tattoos. I'm not surprised she worked that out. The rest, well, I'm not surprised by that either. If you live with your captor long enough, the only way to survive is to convince yourself they're good people. Depending upon when she was taken, this girl might have truly believed Lady Essia helped her," said Bredych as they sat outside the farm house.

"She blamed me, Bredych. Said I'd taken it all away from her and accused me of murder."

Bredych nodded. "Most people will. This calling isn't for the weak of heart. We help those who need it most. We are the Thirteen's protectors. As scholars of the Thirteen, we understand the laws better than non-scholars do. Would you rather those young girls be sold to men as slaves?"

"No, but—"

"There's no but, Shendra. Those girls won't be abandoned. The town will look after them. They will rebuild Tovias, and those girls will have a chance at a real life now. Because of us."

Her brother was so convinced. His eyes glowed with the belief that he served Justice, the belief in something greater than himself, and she envied him his ignorance.

He glanced at the sky where the clouds were clearing. "We should head out soon. The Order will be waiting for our report."

They'd be waiting for her answer.

If it was too late now to back out, perhaps she could change the Order. Maybe they didn't have to be contract killers. There had to be other ways of serving Justice...

THEIR REPORTS WERE GIVEN TO THE AMASKAN MASTERS separately, each giving a detailed account of what happened, why they thought it happened, and what actions and decisions could've been improved upon. It was the latter that left Shendra tongue-tied as she found herself floundering in guilt. While Master Elish asked questions intended to derive the facts from her, he gave no indication of whether or not her guilt was warranted. His face remained an expressionless mask as he took down the accountings.

After she'd relayed the details of the job, he asked, "Do you wish to be an Amaskan?"

A simple question—one she'd pondered over the entire journey home—and yet, her stomach churned when he asked it. Finally, she spoke. "I do."

"Why?"

It shouldn't have been unexpected, yet it was, and she swallowed the bile at the back of her throat. "As Amaskans, we're imperfect. We work in the service of Justice, but we're not gods. We don't know if someone's guilty. So we research and investigate. We do the best we can to help others, which is all anyone can do. Bredych has this way about 'im like he knows some secret truth. Like everythin' he does is right."

"And you don't?"

"No, Master. But I believe the Order is tryin' to do what's right the best way they can. I'm nineteen. I have a lot to learn still 'bout life and Justice. Maybe my doubts come from lack of wisdom."

Master Elish tilted his head. "So you admit to having doubts?"

Shendra didn't want to answer, but while traveling home, she'd promised herself to be honest. If the gods wanted her to serve, she would serve. If her truth kept her from that, it would be Their decision and not hers. "Everyone should have doubts. If we don't, we ain't thinkin' enough 'bout what we're doin'."

"And your wish to change the Order?"

Her cheeks grew warm. It was a thought she'd shared with Bredych, one not intended for their Master's hearing. Of course her brother had shared it. He was loyal to the Order.

"I still wish it. I wish only to improve us in seekin' Justice for those who need it."

He glanced to his left where the other Masters sat in stony silence. "*Some* believe nineteen is too young to be an Amaskan. Most trainees do not become journeymen members until later in life. You, yourself, have commented on how emotional this test was for you with how close it has been to your past. Do you feel you are ready to join the Order, Shendra? There is no shame in training further."

"I'm ready."

Master Elish nodded, his face relaxed, yet smooth and expressionless. "You may wait in the hall."

With no indication of how her test had gone from her master or the others, she sat on a stone bench outside, her body too tense to feel the stone beneath her. No one had commented on the magic or the *chathula's* existence, nor had they questioned Lady Essia's use of it.

Those conversations would happen behind closed doors without her, and for once, she was glad of the fact.

Bredych had followed her report with his, which took twice as long as her own. By the time the doorknob moved, her stress had shifted to hunger and fatigue. She stood up as her brother, head down, exited the room. Before she could call out to him, Master Elish gestured for her to follow him inside.

Now that the report had been made, many smiles greeted her as she entered the room. The masters gathered at a long table that sat behind two chairs, the ones she and her master had used during her report. Frowns decorated a face or two, especially once Master Elish turned both chairs to be included in the circle rather than facing each other.

"Take your seat, please," he said, and she claimed it with a slight tremble.

Did the smiles and chair turning mean she'd made it? Or was it intended to put her off guard?

"Shendra Abner of Sadai, you have sat the training for entrance into the Order of Amaska, a most sacred calling serving Justice before all, is this correct?"

"I-It is."

"Shendra Abner of Sadai, have you successfully completed your test?" asked Master Elish.

Technically she had. Her tongue thickened in her mouth. "I-I have."

Master Elish smiled as he glanced at the other masters. "It is with this knowledge that I recommend Shendra Abner of Sadai be granted entrance into the Order of Amaska."

A woman near the sun's age shook her head, her wrinkled face bunching up as she peered at Shendra. "The girl's brother doesn't think she's ready. What have you to say to that?"

It was a punch to the gut, and she bit her lip to keep the emotion from her face. *Not ready? When did he think that?*

"Her brother worries about her doubts, but I say it is Amaskan Bredych who is not ready—not ready to seek the position he does. He believes fiercely and is loyal to a fault, but he fails to see the long plan. Shendra seeks to serve Justice and ensure we all do to the best of our abilities. It is natural to doubt—"

"We've heard this, Elish," the old woman said and pointed at Shendra. "I want to know what *she* thinks."

"A-about what, Master?"

"About your brother's lack of trust in your abilities."

Shendra swallowed hard as sweat rolled down her back. "I don't have an answer for that. Perhaps it's what Master Elish has said—my brother sees my natural questionin' and doubt as a weakness rather than a strength."

The old woman raised an eyebrow, but tilted her head to Master Elish. "Any other questions for this trainee?" he asked, and when no one spoke up, he smiled. "Rise, trainee."

Shendra stood, her shoulders square and legs straight, though one knee trembled for a moment.

"Formerly Trainee Shendra Abner of Sadai, the Masters have voted and you are being granted membership into the Order of Amaska. Hence, from now forward, you are Journeyman Shara of Amaska."

The hot needle glowed, the color reminding her of Tovias, and her eyes widened. Master Elish seized the needle, though he paused at the scabbed over wound on her jaw. "This must be the mark you spoke of."

"Yes, Master."

"Let us give you a proper mark."

Like a cat scratch on fire, the needle burned as it marked her flesh with a circle—infinite wisdom given to Justice by the Gods themselves. So focused was she on the mark that she almost didn't feel it when the sharp knife swept across her head, shearing the hair from her. Waves of black fell to the floor as someone stepped forward and shoved a wad of cotton into her hand.

"Hold this against the wound."

She followed the instruction, expecting something soothing, but instead, the mark on her jaw stung and her eyes watered in response.

"Now this one."

Shendra—now Shara—followed this instruction slower, but discovered it was the aloe she'd been expecting. A few more passes and her head was bare like everyone else.

For better or worse, this was her family and had been since she was fifteen years old. Perhaps she would make it better. Perhaps she would die trying.

After all, she was an Amaskan.

She served no one but Justice.

But first, she was going to have a conversation with that brother of hers...

ABOUT "AMASKAN"

Originally published in *Hidden Magic: Magical Unground Anthology 1* (Magical Mayhem Press), "Amaskan" is a story intended to shed more light on the background of Ida Warhammer from *Amaskan's Blood*. At the time of writing, I wasn't planning to write a novel on her backstory, so the short story served the purpose of giving the readers her origin story so to speak.

# PEACE BE WITH YOU, FRIEND

In the early days of Litalle's life, the sun climbed the sky to provide warmth, sometimes more than was required. That same sun buried itself beneath the horizon each evening, giving life a chance to cool off beneath twin moons. *Sleep* and *rejuvenation* were words worth knowing, as were *family* and *friends* and *community*.

But with each year that passed, the haze outside her village engulfed an increasing amount of blue, leaving behind a sky of ash and ice. This annual eclipse shifted to seasons and then to months as Litalle's words gave way to terms like *hunger* and *thirst* and *loneliness*.

Words carried power, or they had before people stopped using them altogether. Solar flares rendered the world useless until her sun waned. Breezes that had once carried cherry blossoms and marigolds, stilled, leaving stagnation in their wake. Speaking became dangerous, even with face masks.

Somewhere in Litalle's memories remained words like *Mother* and *best friend,* but both figures had died back when the summer rivers froze. She'd been sixteen when their deaths added two coats to her young shoulders. More to carry and a burden at first, but now...

Litalle tugged the coats tighter about her shoulders as she shivered. With each death in her village, she'd inherited what remained: a few scraps of food, a canteen of water, clothing riddled with holes, and sometimes their last words.

"Luck be with you, friend."

Somewhere during the village's drawn-out death, days bled together as the gray and white permeated everything. Maybe she'd left its remains a few days before her eighteenth birth year, a rather solemn event celebrated not at all, with strangers at her side. Now nineteen—at least she thought that might've be her age—she walked across the land with no direction, no company, and no purpose beyond staying alive.

Four hundred days since her last encounter with a living person. Four days since her last encounter with a living animal. Four hours ago, she'd uncovered a dragonfly nymph settled beneath the frozen pond while filling her canteen, a tidbit to be tucked into her backpack for later.

She glanced at the gray sun in the distance. One hand, maybe two above the horizon, gave her an hour until the sun slept. Maybe tonight would be the night it finally died. Litalle shrugged as she climbed up the hill.

A chilly wind sent the forest's dried up limbs clattering like an old set of bamboo wind chimes. Their hollow, mournful cries forced her steps faster. The tree remnants shivered with her, and when they stilled, darkness hovered beneath their empty canopy. A cave or an overhang? She hoped for the former.

Her fingers curled tighter around her crossbow as she tiptoed towards the shadows. Rather than a slight overhang of branches, the trees gave way to a large cave—large enough that the rear of it was lost to more shadows. Taller than her by two, its mouth promised shelter, but she swallowed back the urge to rush inside. If she sought shelter from the night, so did others, assuming anyone or anything else was alive to do so. If bullets remained for her gun, perhaps her limbs would tremble less, but the last time she'd stumbled upon spare bullets, the stench of death surrounding them had driven her away.

Something glinted within the blackness, and she slowed her steps. She remained silent and still, and when nothing happened, she opened her mouth. At first, nothing sounded other than a slight croak. So long had it been since she'd spoken, and she swallowed hard.

"H-Hello?"

This time a light alto rang out and bounced around the cave, too loud for ears used to silence, and she clapped a dirty hand over her chapped lips.

Whatever inhabited the cave flickered but remained present. She unclipped her flashlight from her belt and cranked its handle a few times to give it juice. Light hit the side of the cave, and as she walked, several somethings flickered ahead of her, their golden hue like autumn leaves back when the seasons shifted and green still grew. Beneath her feet, a deep rumble shook her, and she stopped, shining her light straight ahead. Her mouth fell open.

A dragon.

Not just any dragon, but a bone-thin, scaley dragon. He enveloped gold in his wings as he watched her, and when she didn't flee, he grinned a mouth full of yellowed, sharp teeth.

"Greetings, child. Or I believe you to be a child. So bundled are you that scarcely an ounce of you shows. Is it the cold you fear, or do you disguise your wealth beneath such covers?"

"Cold, sir. I lack your wonderous scales to keep me warm." She pushed several scarves aside to better show her gaunt face. When her stomach grumbled audibly, the dragon's tongue flicked the air.

"How fortunate for me that you have stumbled upon my home, here at the end of time." His voice's deep rumble set her knees and the trees outside to rattling.

"My name is Litalle, sir." Though she bowed her head as was proper, she kept her eyes on his feet. She'd never outrun a dragon proper, but this one being half-starved...perhaps she could lose him in the dead forest. "I meant no harm, sir. I only sought this cave as shelter for the evening."

The dragon spread out his claws and gold coins skittered across the cave's floor. He remained firmly on his hoard. "My name is long forgotten, child, though it matters not. Tonight the sun will wither and die, and the land will fall into permanent slumber. Perhaps if I am to join it, I would do so with a full belly. Come here, child."

His attempt to give her his name was close enough to meeting protocol, and she dared meet his gaze. If he took offense, it hardly mattered if he spoke the truth about the world ending. Either way she'd die. The thought nearly took her breath away as she stared at the dragon. "Are you not content to pass into the Everlands with your riches?" she asked.

"I can't eat gold, child, and my belly rumbles as much as yours. Maybe more. Here at the end of the world, at the end of time itself, all this gold has given me is a crick in the neck. But you? You shall make my belly warm again."

As the dragon slid one shaky foot to the ground, she held up both hands. Eyes wide, she called out, "But, sir, I'm barely an appetizer. You'd eat me and find yourself hungrier rather than sated."

He tilted his head at her, his green eyes glinting yellow in light. Her flashlight flickered as its battery screamed for energy, and she gave it a quick crank.

Don't die. Not now.

"Sir, I've heard it said that dragons hold the knowledge of the world, of all Tarrah, and if that's true and the end is truly nigh, would it not be better to die in the warmth of a good fire with a...f-friend rather than fighting an enemy over a tiny morsel?"

The dragon eyed her flashlight and laughed. "Your tiny light dies even as we speak."

"True, but if you promise not to eat me, I'll make us a large fire where we can be warm together. The trees outside are as dead as we will be and would burn nicely. I'd be honored to use this fire to make us a proper, fulfilling meal."

He sniffed the air, then stepped forward to sniff at her backpack. Whatever scent he found gave him pause, and as the sun crawled closer to the horizon, the dragon gave a single nod. "I know not what a friend is, but if you can make me a proper meal, perhaps I won't eat you. Perhaps we can be this...friend you speak of."

Litalle's hands trembled as she turned her back on the dragon. No hot breath ruffled her hair, nor did anything sharp render her end-to-end. The dragon had kept his word thus far, and she shuffled outside into the trees. She could run... Maybe she'd make it down the hill before the starving dragon found the energy to catch her, or maybe he'd let her leave, knowing that the cold would kill her without any effort at all.

She spied glowing green flickers now and again watching her from the cave as she collected a large bundle of tree branches, much larger than she would normally gather. Several trips inside the cave brought them something more bonfire than fire pit, and she used her emergency fire starter to light the kindling. The clacking of dragon claws made her smile as he approached the flames, though her smile faltered as she glimpsed ribs prominently displayed through almost translucent scales.

The dragon really was starving to death.

Her fingers dug their way through the layers of clothing she wore until ice cold, they found her skin. She bit her lip as she counted the ribs that ran across her own frame. So similar and yet so different.

The dragon curled his body around the warmth like a kitten, and then tapped one claw on the ground. "I will wait here for your fine meal."

Inside her backpack, various bits of food and survival gear swam in a large pot. She hadn't needed it in ages—not enough food to warrant its use—but she fetched it now, upending the last of her water supplies into it, along with the dragonfly nymph, some dried jerky bits, and a few frozen worms. As the dragon watched, she scooped up a few gold coins and tossed them in for good measure. When the dragon arched a brow at her, she said, "It's for flavor."

Maybe it would fool him, but in truth, the pot held little more than flavored water. It held everything she had, and she shivered. If the dragon was wrong and the world continued beyond tonight, she'd have nothing to eat or drink come morning. Provided the dragon didn't eat her. But if the dragon was right...

For a moment, her mother's words rippled through her mind and swept away all doubt. "If you are ever so lucky as to encounter a dragon, know this—they are the masters of all knowledge. They see what has been and what will be, so treat them with dignity before you flee back to me!"

As she stirred the soup, Litalle allowed her mind to drift. Better that than fear. So many had gone before her. How'd she out-survive them? Was it luck, or was she unlucky, left alone to see the end and its approach? For all that the dragon scared her, at least she wasn't alone.

She pulled her thermal jacket closer about her shoulders, the one with the hole in the pocket that her mother had worn worrying its edge. Its zipper had long since failed, but its woolen insides still added warmth to the other layers.

The sun froze against the horizon as Litalle scooped a small portion of soup into her cup before passing the entire pot to the dragon. While she sipped hers in near silence, the dragon slurped the broth with a recognizable desperation.

When the pot was cleaned of every droplet, the dragon set his short arms on his belly and shook his wings once before curling up again beside the fire. "What magic was that, child?"

"Magic?"

"That soup was both filling and tasty. Was it the gold? Did I have food beside me this entire time?" Before she could answer, the dragon picked up a gold coin between his claws and tossed it into his gaping gullet. His sharp teeth made quick work of the old coin, but upon swallowing, he frowned. "This tastes nothing like your soup."

Litalle's limbs felt heavy as she shuffled closer to both the fire and the dragon. "No magic. If I had magic, I'd summon a grander feast than this, I promise."

The dragon blinked slowly at her as the bitter cold crept its way across the cave, and the fire shuddered in response. "Then I ask again, what magic is this that turns a few grubs into such a meal?"

"Friendship," she said as scooted between the fire and the dragon. When he remained in place, she leaned against his belly for warmth. It was a foolish move perhaps, but as frost gathered on her brows and eyelashes, she snuggled as close as she could to his warm scales.

"What is friendship?"

When the dragon said the word, he frowned. Perhaps it didn't taste the same on his tongue as it did on hers, and she tilted her head in thought. The cold fatigued her mind, but after a long moment, she smiled. "Before all this, there were other dragons on Tarrah, right?"

When he nodded, she asked, "Were there any that you lived with?"

"There might have been one. A green little thing who spun rain in the spring and gave me an egg in the summer."

"You had offspring?"

The dragon nodded. "She was the first to die. We...we were very hungry."

Litalle suppressed a shudder. "Where there any others?"

"At one time. We would hunt together on the Hills of Horick and chase sheep across the plains."

"That sounds very much like a friend," she said. Her eyes grew heavy as the air grew thin, and the sun's light faded one last time. "We've both been alone for s-so long. Any meal flavored with h-hunger and friendship will taste like f-fresh made bread and wine."

A deep rumble sounded within the dragon as he wrapped his massive tail about her. "Perhaps you are right. Perhaps you are a...friend. After all, you brought a warm light and a fine meal to one who would've eaten you."

"And you've provided warmth and conversation in return. If it's the end, let us fade together, sir."

Another rumble of agreement as outside, life fell silent.

THE GIRL IN HIS ARMS FELL ASLEEP FIRST AS THE FROST creeping across the cave floor thickened. When her breath stopped, the dragon licked her face.

"I could eat you now. You'd never know. But I did promise that I wouldn't..."

Ice as thick as his wrists covered his scales and his wings, which he could no longer spread. He curled his claws around the girl to form a protective circle about her and grinned.

"'Twas a fine meal, child."

The firelight faded along with the heat, and the dragon's lids fell heavily across his glittering eyes. "Goodnight, Litalle. May we rest well. Luck be with us, *friend*."

This time when he said the word, it hummed with power. The sound and the cold lulled the dragon to sleep, the hum only fading when Tarrah heaved its last, cold breath.

"*...end.*"

ABOUT "PEACE BE WITH YOU"

Originally published as an e-Book, this is my short story at the end of the world. I wanted to write about two unlikely friends, together as the world dies around them. What would they have to talk about? Would they kill each other over the last bit of food? I really enjoy this story and like to hope this would be humanity's way of dealing with the end of Earth.

# THE SNARK

There once was a young woman who epitomized the snark of a dozen Redditers—oh who was she kidding? It was more like a thousand if she did say so herself. PixieMe, or Elizabeta Wallace as it read on her birth certificate, dwelled in a maze of twisted cat6's and binary digits where she rallied her keyboard warriors to a mouth-foaming frenzy over such topics as "Why *Do* We Pay For Health Care If We're Healthy?" and "Why Isn't Gigabit Internet a Constitutional Right?"

Be it noon or the hour reserved for the Late Show with Stephen Colbert, her gaze never wavered from the masses in need of some snide advice. At least not until yesterday morning when a fist-sized hole appeared in her lair—a hole as dark as her eyeliner and as damp as a newbie's pits with their first comment to Fark. How perfect her basement lair had been: a custom rig sporting dual video cards, quad-core processors, and four thirty-inch monitors mounted across the back wall. Toss in her vibrating gamer chair with Bluetooth, some wireless peripherals, and Gigabit Internet, and PixieMe was ready to paint the world with her brand of sarcasm.

But then the hole had appeared.

Three fireballs into a campaign, her group lost to a level ten centaur.

"WTH? Did you suddenly grow fat fingers or do you always roll that low?" she typed, then grinned when the rest of the party joined in. The smell of moist soil and rotted pork assaulted her real-life nose, and she turned to find herself eye-level with the hole. While PixieMe was a perpetual badass online and quite prone to sticking her nose in other people's business, her real-life self was anything but. Whose business *was* this? What right did it have to be in *her* domain?

No cross-beams or insulation—just a hub full of moist, hot air. Much like people online.

Brown bits of rags she'd tossed in the garbage last week flashed across the opening, and she thrust her hand in after it, catching a wrinkle of cloth by its corner. It wasn't the popping sound her fist made exiting the hole that startled her, but the dirty-little-man sporting knotted rags, feathers, and whiskers.

"What the hell are you?" PixieMe asked. She would've dropped the creature, but he'd wrapped his stubby little arms around her bleeding finger like an Assassin Vine constricting wild boar for fertilizer.

He opened his mouth and chittered at her, and she shook her finger until the noise stopped.

"I *said*, What. The. Hell. Are. You."

"Whadaya think? Imma Snark."

She tugged on the green twist-tie holding his cellophane wings to his body. "More like the garbage man, amiright?"

Over the headset, someone shouted for her while another player cursed her character.

"Looks like I'll be sweepin' up your character with today's trash," the Snark said. His whiskers tickled her fingers when he grinned.

PixieMe flicked one of his wings, but when she opened her mouth to let loose a snide remark, he slashed her thumb with pointed fingernails.

"O—!" She tried to cry out, but the words fell from her tongue. Her lungs still worked. Her tongue still moved and swallowing was still allowed, but no sound emitted from her lips. PixieMe dropped the Snark on her desk and turned to her keyboard. She'd meant for her fingers to press the shortcut for Notepad, but the moment they touched the keys, her fingertips swelled to the size of ripe cherries.

*Farthsibarght*, she typed. *FARTHSIBARGHT!*

Thrice more she typed, and thrice more, her words were gibberish. PixieMe stared at the Snark, her bottom lip thrust out in a pout.

"Really? You think that will work?"

She nodded her head, and the Snark laughed.

He laughed as he fluttered off her desk. He laughed as he flew to the hole. His chittering and chortling followed him as he retreated into the darkness.

Her eyeliner ran down her cheeks and sweat tickled her pits as she tried without success to communicate. Her fingertips shrink, and her voice return to her—albeit with a lighter, less snark-filled sound.

Someone yelled in game and when she unmuted her mic, she said, "I love you, too! You have a good, safe game now, you hear?"

Her mouth fell open. That hadn't been at all what she'd intended to say, so she tried again. "This game is a bit violent. Is anyone up for a nice board game?"

Laughter filled her ears and she tossed her headphones aside. No matter how much she tried, nothing impolite left her brain, be it through her fingers or her mouth.

One final laugh escaped the gaping hole nearby, and when she glanced at it, the Snark gave her a final wink before disappearing again.

The hole shrank until it was no more.

## About "The Snark"

Ah, yes, this little tale. "The Snark" is my story of the ultimate payment for the snarky trolls on the Internet. There's not much more to say than that! Maybe that payback's a bitch.

# DRAGON SPRINGS & OTHER THINGS

"A dragon? Why a dragon?

"The real question is why not a dragon. I mean, can't you see it?" I asked.

My father frowned, his bushy brows climbing further towards his receding hairline.

"No, no—just picture it! Robo-wings in gold stretched out across the blue skies of Gharmon. What a sight. Everyone would love it!"

My father sighed. "Now Jonna, wouldn't this time off from your studies be better spent developing something of...well, better use? Perhaps fixing the plumbing at the academe or working on that new steam powered contraption—that rolling thing. What did Bron call it?"

"A train, Father," I muttered and repressed the urge to roll my eyes.

"Yes, the train. Why can't you make something like that? His Majesty would be sure to notice us—your work."

"Just what I need. Another man telling me what to do."

"What is that supposed to mean?"

I waved a roughened hand in the air. He wouldn't understand even if I tried to explain it.

"Besides, what would you make a dragon out of?"

I grinned. It was a question I'd contemplated for years, ever since I'd been apprenticed to Bron. "Springs and...well, other things you wouldn't understand—it doesn't matter. I've got the plans drafted and a space in Bron's workshop ready to go...."

He leveled a new stern glare. "I had hoped you were beyond such... frivolous ventures, Jonna. You're fifteen and 'prenticed to one of the best tinkerers in the kingdom. It's a high honor, not one to be taken lightly or squandered away on a fantastical nothing."

"But a dragon would be a boon to the crown! A guardian and means of travel both. Imagine, Father—flying!"

"And crashing to the rocky ground below. Dead. What would I do if I lost you?" His voice trembled as he spoke, and he gripped my shoulder tightly.

Have to make your own tea for once.

"Promise me you'll put your time to something more worthwhile. Something...safer."

A picture of the train popped into my head. Twelve people had lost limbs developing it—a fact my father either ignored or was not aware of —and I nodded. What he didn't know wouldn't hurt him.

At least not yet.

I HAD NEGLECTED TO TELL MY FATHER THAT BRON WAS traveling, and I'd have the workshop all to myself. As far as he was concerned, I spent the majority of my time slaving over the train everyone in the village was waiting to see. Instead, I came up dirty and greasy from time digging through scrap mounds for anything and everything. I'd built enough robotic birds to understand the necessary gears, springs, and metal slab needed, though I burned myself thrice when using the welder. Last time, Bron had held the pieces for me as I used the machine. With him gone, I needed more hands than I physically had and for a moment, I contemplated creating a third arm. With something like that, I could create twice as fast...

Without blueprints, I'd never succeed. Besides, something in my gut told me the King wouldn't approve, and I set the idea aside as I continued work on my dragon. Something large, but not so large I couldn't ride it. After all, if it was to fly, I wanted to be the first one to try it. The town blacksmith had a good supply of scrap from a job gone sideways, which he was glad to shove off on me if it meant I had to haul it back to the workshop myself. Donating it to the tinkerers also meant he wouldn't have to pay a fine for wasted metal.

Three days of gathering what I needed and another three was all it took to build him, a polished beast of silver and bronze, standing about four meters tall with wings that spread out from their ball joints like a proper flying creature. There wasn't much I could do about the visible gears as he lacked any proper skin in most areas that moved, but he was beautiful all the same.

His on switch, a small toggle on his belly, lay waiting for me, and my finger hovered over it for a solid minute. Why couldn't I flip it on? What was I waiting for?

"Jonna? Are you in there?"

My father's voice started me, and I tossed a dirty blanket over the dragon's head before stepping outside the workroom. When I closed the door behind me, my father's brows furrowed.

"I thought you were working with Bron on the train?"

"I am. He has me building a particular engine piece for it. It's all hush-hush, so you shouldn't even be here."

He laughed deep from his belly. "I came here to see if you were coming home anytime soon. It's nearly morning, and you're the only one here."

My jaw fell open. Was it really so late? "I-I'm sorry, Father. I guess I lost track of time."

He ruffled my mop of hair with a grin. "Ya definitely take after your mother. Tinkerer to your toes."

I followed him from the workshop with a sigh. My dragon would have to wait.

I woke to the sound of screaming. Lots of screaming. My father beat me to the door by a gear's width, though he was still tugging his boots on. Falling asleep fully dressed has its advantages, though he crinkled his nose at me as we opened the door. Our town was small, one of three leading up to the castle, with one main road dividing it. Outside, the entire town gathered by a woman whose finger shook as she pointed skyward.

At first, I wondered if she'd had too much drink when she shouted again, but when I glanced up, my stomach leapt into my throat. A dragon—*my dragon*—flew overhead.

"How—"

My father clapped a hand over my mouth. "Shush now. Don't make a scene."

*How did it turn on? Who found it and more importantly, why was everyone afraid?*

It turned on a wingtip toward town and dove. The crowd before us scattered as they shouted, and my dragon flapped his wings a few times as it landed in the town square. I stepped forward when my father's hand clamped on my shoulder. "But—"

He leaned close to my ear. "If the town finds out you made it, there'll be questions and problems. Look at how scared they are."

All around me people grabbed weapons, be they pots or sticks, and they gathered a decent distance away to defend their homes. My dragon chirped and a small speck of flame escaped his mouth.

"You gave him fire?" my father hissed.

I shrugged. What self-respecting dragon *wouldn't* have flames?

Between one moment and the next, our blacksmith stepped forward, hammer in hand. He swung it towards my dragon, who sidestepped the hit. Another burst of flame, this one much larger, escaped the dragon's mouth.

"Stop! He's just afraid!" I shouted, but no one listened.

A few stones landed on his metal body, and he roared. The ground shook with the deep sound, and this time when he let loose his flame, he pointed it in the direction of a dwelling. The thatch roof caught immediately, and when I turned back to my dragon, he was gone.

"There." My father pointed into the sky where my dragon was disappearing into the trees of the nearby forest.

"I have to find him."

This time, my father didn't stop me as I ran. When I returned, good news or bad, a lecture awaited me for sure. With hope my "train" didn't burn the entire town down. I'd never hear the end of it.

WHILE I WAS USED TO CRAWLING THROUGH BITS OF METAL and cast-aside machinery, tromping through the woods wasn't something I was used to as branches and twigs caught my shirt and pants as I passed. In my hurry, I'd left without my cloak, and the morning chill set my teeth to chattering.

His warning growl reached me before I spotted my dragon, and when I stepped into the small clearing, his eyes shifted from a deep blue to green and back again. A tiny puff of smoke escaped his nostrils, but otherwise he sat facing me, waiting.

"I'm so sorry. They didn't know you were scared. They thought you meant to hurt them." I spoke but he gave no indication that he understood me, and I sighed. "Can—can I approach?"

I took one step forward, then another when he remained still. My dragon watched me and while his eyes held intelligence, he didn't answer. Maybe he couldn't. Maybe the speech center wasn't working. I reached out a hand to touch him, and he leaned back.

"I won't hurt you, promise."

It was the same metal I used to build him, but something about his snout felt different, almost alive. When I leaned to look at his sides, they moved.

Inhale. Exhale.

I stumbled backward and tripped over my boots.

My dragon whined when I hit the ground, eyes rapidly swirling a sharp blue. He nosed my legs and snorted.

He was breathing. Machines didn't need to breathe. I studied the metal of his face as it reflected the sunlight like metal should, but it also rippled. The pieces of him flowed like skin as he moved.

"You're alive. That's how you turned on. Because you're alive!"

This time when I touched him, I ran my fingers under his chin and he crooned. He couldn't speak, but he didn't need to. "Stay here," I told him. "I-I need to explain things to the townspeople so they won't hurt you, okay? It'll be safe here."

My dragon settled down on his haunches, tail and wings wrapped around him like a shield.

"It'll be safe here. Stay."

*I think.*

I backed out of the clearing cautiously, but once away from my dragon's gaze, I ran for all I was worth. He was alive! My dragon lived!

ONE HOME LAY IN RUBBLE WHEN I RETURNED TO TOWN AND A few others lacked roofs. Though the stench of smoke and soot remained, the flames were gone. My father spotted me and gestured for me to follow him into our home.

He closed the door behind me. "Did you find the creature?"

"Yes. Father, he's alive!"

"A well-designed machine should move like it's living. I'd be surprised if anything you made did naught else."

My hands froze at my side. "How—?"

"You think me a simpleton, Jonna, because I'm not a tinkerer, but I lived with one for twenty years before your mother passed. You think I can't understand the way your mind works? The draw of creating something no one else has? What I don't understand is why you set it loose on the town!" His voice rose as he spoke until the last sentence, which hurt my ears with its volume.

"I didn't! That's what I'm trying to tell you."

He shook his head. "Look, they've sent a message to the King. The guards will be here soon to slay the beast before it does any more damage. It would be better if you tell no one you created it and let it loose."

"Wait, the Royal Guards? But he's just a young dragon. He was scared. They hurt him with the rocks and...he didn't mean to burn down a house. Please, Father, you can't let them kill him. He's alive. Not just a machine, but actually alive."

His hand gripped my shoulder. "Do as you're told, Jonna. Stay inside and don't speak of this beast again."

The door slammed as he left and a wooden cup fell from a nearby wall shelf. My dragon awaited me in the woods. I'd told him it was safe. My mind whirled, and when I looked out the window, my father spoke with the blacksmith. Had he recognized the metal I'd taken from him? Did he know who created the dragon?

When the blacksmith glanced toward our home, he met my gaze straight on, and I backed away, allowing the simple curtain to fall back into place. When I took a second glance, both men had turned toward the square where our runner stood, chest heaving. He held a parchment in his hands bearing dark ink. Even from this distance I could see the King's mark on the bounty.

I tore through the front door, not bothering to close it on my way out, and stopped near the back of the crowd.

"King Edwin has declared a ten silver reward for information related to this beast. Thirty silver for anyone who can rid us of it."

"He ain't sendin' the guards?" asked the baker.

The runner shook his head. "Guessing he figures with a reward, he won't have to."

I inched back from the group until I stood beside our door. Once inside, I glanced in the small mirror that hung on the wall. Dirt smudged my nose and leaves clung to my shirt. There was no chance I could gain entrance to see the King looking like I did, but the longer I dallied, the higher the chances that my dragon would die. I rubbed the corner of a curtain across my face and brushed at my clothes.

It would have to do.

By the time my father noticed his missing horse and daughter, I'd be at the castle and under the watchful eye of the guards. Or so I hoped. When I approached the forest clearing, my dragon lay still, his eyes closed. His nostrils twitched as he recognized my scent, but otherwise, he remained relaxed and resting.

"Dragon, I-I have to go to the castle now. There are people coming for you, and I need to explain that you aren't dangerous. Is there somewhere you could hide? Somewhere safer than here?" I asked.

He stood, stretching first his legs and then his wings, before he launched into the skies. Whether he understood all of my words or not, he recognized the warning in my voice. I returned to my "borrowed" horse and set off towards the castle.

"Halt!" The guardsman held up his hand as I approached. He walked up to me and frowned. "What business do you have here?"

"I hear there's a reward for information on the Beast."

"There is. Are you hear to report such information?"

When I nodded, he took the reins from me and led me in through the castle gates.

"Let's have it then," he said as I dismounted.

"The information is for His Majesty only."

His slick smile was as slimy as his figure, and I stood my ground. When I didn't react to his breath in my face, he sighed and called for someone up on the wall. A moment or two later, a broad shouldered guard with a fair number of facial scars approached. "What news, Garreth?" he asked.

"Little runt says she has information on the beast."

"Did you ask her what it was?"

Garreth laughed, a vile sound that made my skin crawl. "Says it's only for *His Majesty*."

The broad shouldered guard nodded, then glanced at me. "Have her horse seen to, Garreth."

He frowned, but did what he was told while his superior gestured for me to follow him. We cut across a courtyard and into the castle proper where no one stopped us until we reached a lengthy hallway towards the castle's center. The set of guards here wore armor that shined like my dragon, and my stomach clenched.

"We have information for His Majesty regarding the beast."

*We. As if he had anything to do with my creation.* While I often spoke my mind, much to the annoyance of everyone, I kept my mouth shut. I needed to speak to the King, which meant remaining silent for the time being. When the guards looked me up and down, I bit my tongue until I tasted blood.

They seated us in a waiting area until a few minutes later, we were ushered into a audience chamber. I'd only seen pictures of King Edwin, which were apparently based on his younger years as wrinkles and moles decorated his face now. His graying hair fell in thin waves above his shoulders and his crown was nearly embedded into his fat head. The guardsman knelt and I followed his example.

"You bring news of the beast?"

Too hollow a voice for a man of such size.

The guardsman nudged me, and I stood. "Yes, Your Majesty."

"Don't keep us waiting, girl. This is a dangerous creature!"

"Yes, Your Majesty, I mean, no, Your Majesty. It isn't dangerous at all." My voice shook as he stared down at me from his dais. "I-I mean, the dragon, he...he's something I made."

King Edwin's eyes narrowed. "You made such a foul creature?"

"Yes, Your Majesty. I thought it would be a boon to the kingdom. Something that could help—"

He held up a hand to stop me. "You are a tinkerer, yes? Apprenticed to whom?"

"Master Bron, Your Majesty."

"And this Bron knows of your creation?"

I shook my head.

"I see. Does anyone else know of your foolishness?"

"My father, but only afterward. Only once it landed in our town."

The King turned towards the guardsman beside me. "This would be Gharmon, the town that sent the runner this morning?"

"Yes, Your Majesty. Apparently it burned down some of the town."

"But he didn't mean to!" I shouted before quickly adding the honorific. "He was scared. He landed in town because he saw me and when some of the townsfolk threw rocks at him, he defended himself. He wasn't trying to burn down the town, Your Majesty. He didn't understand."

The King stood, pacing back and forth a few times before he stepped down from his throne. I stared at my feet as he approached me, and when his cold hand lifted my chin, I tried to stare at my own cheeks to keep from seeing him.

"Look at me, child."

My gaze crawled up to meet his automatically, and I held my breath. While I'd thought him old, nothing compared to seeing him up close. He was *ancient*. His wrinkles had wrinkles, but his blue eyes were bright as he stared at me.

"You're Jonna, Ava's daughter?"

I gasped. "You know of my mother, Your Majesty?"

"One of the best tinkerers in the Kingdom. Her loss was great. Now, while I do not think you intended harm, you have created a weapon, something of destruction, that if not controlled, could doom us. Because of this, I order you to bring the creature to me."

My hands clenched at my sides as my eyes widened.

King Edwin shook his head. "You misunderstand my intentions, I think, as I do not wish to kill it, child. This creature is a boon, or it will be when we repair it. Think of how our enemies will flee from such a beast! It will rain fire down on anyone who would harm us."

"But he's alive! He's more than a machine now. He's an innocent creature who knows nothing of war, Your Majesty."

The glee vanished from his eyes, and he held up a finger. "You will do this, by order of your king. Now, go. Find this creature you've created."

When the guardsman led me to my horse, he was polite enough not to comment on my tears.

THE CLEARING WAS EMPTY, AS I'D HOPED, BUT AT THE SAME time, what was I to do? If I didn't come back with my dragon, would I be held for treason? Would my father lose his business? A million thoughts ran through my mind until a downdraft of wind touched my hair. I spun around to find my dragon landing in front of me, his mouth turned downward.

I rushed forward and wrapped my arms around his extended neck. For a moment, it was the two of us alone. We could run. We could flee together, somewhere no one would find us, but as the thought crossed my mind, I shook my head. There was no where we could go that someone wouldn't see him. He was the only one of his kind.

"I'm so sorry," I whispered as I stroked his neck. "The King, he's ordered me to bring you to him. He wants to make you a weapon, something used to kill. Do you understand that word? Kill?"

A low rumble escaped him, along with a puff of smoke. He stepped back toward a large boulder and breathed fire. A tree caught, and he stamped it out before it spread. I glanced at the debris—one burned tree, a charred rock, and dirt as black as night. Then he gave himself a mighty shake.

Springs, gears, and other bits and bobs flung off him to decorate the charred area. He picked up a lengthy spring in his mouth and dropped it into my waiting hands.

"I don't understand."

He glanced at the area he'd burned, and I took a closer look.

"Oh! This looks like when one of Bron's inventions goes wrong. Like when they explode." For a moment, I remembered Bron fleeing the workshop, my mother's body in his arms, and I blinked back tears. "You want me to tell them you're...gone."

The dragon gave me a single, deep nod.

"But...don't you need these pieces?"

If the dragon could have laughed, he would have as his mouth tilted up and his eyes whirled a brilliant emerald green. Then he launched himself in the air. A single roar shook the forest before he flew away.

I gathered the spring closer to me. It was time to lie to my king.

THIS TIME WHEN I APPROACHED THE CASTLE, A GROUP OF guards awaited me. Without the dragon following me, they loosened their grips on their weapons. "Is the beast nearby?" one asked, and I shook my head.

"I need to speak with His Majesty."

As before, I was ushered into a waiting area before gaining access to the audience chamber.

"I hear you have returned empty handed."

"Not entirely, Your Majesty," I said as I held up the spring.

He peered at it as he frowned. "And what is this? I ask you to bring me your weapon and you bring me a spring?"

"I returned to where I left him, Your Majesty, but there was an accident. I-I think he exploded." I didn't have to fake the tears that welled in my eyes. The charred remains resembled my mother's accident too much for that. "There were other bits at the site, some burned areas too. I brought this spring as proof."

King Edwin gestured and a guardsman approached. "Describe this area for us."

It wasn't difficult to explain as the clearing was the only large one in the forest beside my town, and once the king felt the guardsman understood my description, he sent him away.

"If he returns and I find that you have lied to me, you will find yourself in more trouble than you know," said King Edwin as he gestured a second time. "While I wait, you can make yourself more comfortable elsewhere."

I was escorted back to the waiting room where I sat, back stiff and fists clenched. The hard wood beneath me wore at me, so I stood and paced the length of the room. The guardsman at the door watched in silence until I lay down on the bench.

"It'll be a while. Get some rest," he said as I closed my eyes.

SOMETHING SHOOK MY SHOULDER, AND WHEN I SAT UP, MY father stood beside me.

"Jonna, I'm so happy to see you safe!"

The guardsman cleared his throat. "I'm sorry, sir, but no one can speak to her now."

"I'm her father! I've come to take her home."

"Not yet, sir. She is in His Majesty's custody until she can be cleared of treason."

My stomach sank. I'd known it likely but hearing it was altogether different—scarier—and I took my father's hand in mine to give it a squeeze.

"I would speak to His Majesty on my daughter's behalf."

The guardsman nodded and behind him, the door opened. Another guard whispered something in his ear, and then they opened the door wide. "His Majesty will see you now, both of you."

The first thing I noticed was the charred bits and pieces from my dragon strewn before the dais, and my father squeezed my hand.

With a frown, the King pointed at the pile. "I would have expected more detritus for such a large beast."

"He wasn't a large dragon, Your Majesty. I made him small enough for me to ride."

"Spoken like a true tinkerer."

My father released my hand and stepped forward. "Your Majesty, I am Aatos, Jonna's father. I promise you she did not understand the consequences of her actions. This tinkering...it puts all sorts of ideas into her head. I can promise that she'll—"

The King wagged a finger at my father. "That sentence better finish with a promise she will continue her apprenticeship."

"I'm sorry, Your Majesty?"

"Your daughter is much like her mother. I suspect she will soon be one of the best tinkerers in the kingdom. A beast like that could have changed the course of the war. If given the proper supplies, what else will her young mind create for us, hmm?"

My father's mouth fell open, then shut with a snap when he recalled his manners.

"Now, my guards have assured me that the beast is destroyed, as she stated, so you may take her home." The King turned his gaze on me. "I'll be keeping an eye on your studies, child. Do your kingdom proud. I don't suppose you happened to make a design on how you made your dragon?"

"No, Your Majesty. I was just tinkering." Another lie, but there was no way I was allowing him or anyone else to try their hand at making a dragon army. I swallowed hard as my king stared at me, then I bowed deeply.

A guardsman cleared his throat, and I followed him out of the audience chamber, my father trailing behind.

Once clear of the castle, I gave him a hug. "I'm sorry, Father."

"Don't apologize. Never apologize when your King honors you."

"But he's gone..."

He placed a finger across my mouth. "And never apologize when you've done the right thing."

"Y-You know?"

My father leaned in close to my ear. "Saw him fly towards the border on my way here."

I gave my father another squeeze. He always knew, and yet, he loved me anyway. "I hope he finds somewhere to be free, somewhere he won't be a weapon."

"Me, too, Jonna, me too. So, what other ideas have you got spinning around in that brain of yours?"

"Oh! Did I tell you about the machine that makes your food?"

He laughed as he helped me mount his horse. "No, but I'm sure you're going to tell me all about it on the ride home, am I right?"

"Yes!" I glanced at the sky once, sure I saw something glint in the sun before I turned off on the road to home.

Fly free, my dragon.

## About "Dragon Springs & Other Things"

I'll be honest, I had the title for this collection of stories before this story existed. I felt the title *Dragon Springs & Other Things* sounded fun and very me in fact. Then I needed a story to go with it. I liked the idea of a young tinkerer who creates something that gets out of hand, something that has a bit of magic of its own. I thought long and hard about how a child or young person would create such a creature. Similar to those rhymes that speak of girls being made of sugar and spice, I wanted a dragon to be made of springs and bits and bops and whatever else could be gathered. What can I say? I love throwing my characters for a loop.

# ACKNOWLEDGMENTS

As usual, I'd like to thank my partner in crime, my always everything, who reads early drafts and gives the best feedback anyone could ask for. Without them, I wouldn't be the writer I am today.

I'd also like to thank the many editors and publishers who first took a chance on publishing some of these stories. I've learned so much from those experiences and can only write better short stories because of those lessons. Special thanks to Janine Southard, Jennifer Brozek, Alesha Escovar, Jeff Cooke, Lee French, Jeff Sturgeon, Sarah Craft, and many others who've chosen my stories for their anthologies, and to Mimi, my editor extraordinaire, who always knows how to make my stories shine.

Once again, the biggest thank you to my readers. I hope these stories bring a little bit of emotion, intrigue, thoughtfulness, and laughter to your day.

# ABOUT THE AUTHOR

Multi-international award-winning speculative fiction author and artist Raven Oak (she/they) is best known for *Amaskan's Blood* (2016 Ozma Fantasy Award Winner, Epic Awards Finalist, & Reader's Choice Award Winner), *Amaskan's War* (2018 UK Wishing Award YA Finalist), and *Class-M Exile*. She also has over a dozen short stories published in anthologies and magazines. She's even published on the moon! (No, really!) Raven spent most of her K-12 education doodling stories and 500-page monstrosities that are forever locked away in a filing cabinet.

Besides being a writer and artist, she's a geeky, disabled ENBY who enjoys getting her game on with tabletop games, indulging in cartography and art, or staring at the ocean. She lives in the Seattle area with her partner, and their three kitties who enjoy lounging across the keyboard when writing deadlines approach. Her hair color changes as often as her bio does, and you can find her at *www.ravenoak.net*.

Do you like what you've read? Want to find out when more books and stories by Raven Oak are released? Want to geek out over the world of science fiction, fantasy, and horror with Raven and other readers?

Then ***Join the Conspiracy***, the official newsletter and reader group for fans of Raven Oak.

If you prefer email updates, you can sign up for *The Conspiracy* newsletter here: https://www.ravenoak.net/join-the-conspiracy/

If you also like discussions, memes, and fun, you can join *The Conspiracy—For Readers of Intriguing Sci-Fi & Fantasy* on Facebook at: https://www.facebook.com/groups/ravenconspiracy/

# ALSO BY RAVEN OAK

<u>The Boahim Universe</u>

*Amaskan's Blood*

*Amaskan's War*

*Amaskan's Honor**

*Ear to Ear**

<u>The Xersian Struggle Universe</u>

*The Eldest Silence**

*Class-M Exile*

<u>Stand-Alone Works</u>

*Ol' St. Nick*

*The Ringers*

*From the Worlds of Raven Oak: A Coloring Book*

*Hungry*

*The Loss of Luna*

*Peace Be With You Friend*

<u>Anthologies</u>

"Not Today" in *99 Fleeting Fantasies* (Pulse Publishing)*

"Drip" in *99 Tiny Terrors* (Pulse Publishing)

"Weightless" in *The Great Beyond Anthology* (BDL Press)

"Scout's Honor" in *The Last Cities of Earth* (Sturgeon Press)

"Amaskan" in *Hidden Magic* (Magical Mayhem Press)

"Pretty Poison" in *Wayward Magic* (Magical Mayhem Press)

"Honor After All" in *Forgotten Magic* (Magical Mayhem Press)

"Alive" in *Swords, Sorcery, & Self-Rescuing Damsels* (Clockwork Dragon Press)

"Mirror Me" 1st edition in *Unveiled Magic* (Creative Alchemy Inc.). 2nd edition published in *Mercedes Lackey Fantasy Quarterly Magazine, Issue 0* (Pulse Publishing)

"Ol' St. Nick" and "The Ringers" 1st edition in *Joy to the Worlds: Mysterious Speculative Fiction for the Holidays* (Grey Sun Press)

"Q-Be" in *Untethered: A Magic iPhone Anthology* (Cantina Publishing)

* Forthcoming

# LIKE WHAT YOU'VE READ?

Word of mouth is the number one **best** way to ensure that your favorite authors have continued success—better than any paid advertisement.

If you enjoyed this book, please consider leaving a **review** or starred ranking on bookstore websites and other retail or reviewer sites. Reviews tell the publisher you want to see more from the author, so help an author out today!

**Your review is greatly appreciated.**